T. N. BAKER

ST. MARTIN'S GRIFFIN ✖ NEW YORK

This is a work of fiction. All of the characters, organizations, and events portrayed in this novel are either products of the author's imagination or are used fictitiously.

Design by Dylan R. Greif

ISBN: 978-0-7394-8623-8

*This book is dedicated to
the loving memory of my father,
Vincent C. Baker.*

ACKNOWLEDGMENTS

Father God, you are my everything! I love you and I thank you for blessing me.

Tiana, you mean the world to me and Mommy loves you so much.

Mother, thank you for being a friend when I need one, you are truly my number one fan, and I thank God for blessing me with you. Love always.

A special thanks to my Grandma, for always holding me down when I'm in need, words can't express how much you mean to me.

To all my sisters and beautiful nieces and nephews. I love you guys!

Badriya, you are my sunshine. God, Mommy loves you so much.

Uncle Antione, thanks for helping me turn my house into a home, that meant a lot to me. Love ya! Uncle Andre, I have nothing but love and respect for you. To all my aunts, cousins, and close friends, thanks for all your love and support. Aunt Jena (Weiner), you've been such a big supporter of my work, I just wanted to let you know I appreciate you, love you, and I'm so proud of you. Joshua, what's up, cuz! I told you I was gonna shout you out.

Vickie Stringer, thank you for believing in T. N. Baker.

St. Martin's Press: Matthew Shear, Anne Marie Tallberg, Kia Dupree, and the sales team, I thank all of you. Monique Patterson, you are the best editor I have ever worked with. This book took me longer than either of us expected but I thank you for your patience and understanding. Much luv!

Maxine Thompson, thanks for your input, and good luck with all your endeavors.

To all of the authors out there doing their thing, I wish you all much success. Danielle Santiago, thanks for being a real friend. Joylynn, it was nice to meet you again in ATL. Mark Anthony, I see you're at the top of your game, thank you so much for being such a wonderful person. Much love and success to you and to QBoro Books! Moye of Inclusive Photography by Moye, thanks for the beautiful photos. You are a force to be reckoned with. See you at the top. *Borderline Magazine* 2007!!! To my boy wise, I wish you nothing but success, much luv! *www.Hoodcelebrities.com*.

A special thanks to the King of New York radio, Ed Lover, for showing me so much love. Queens is in the Building!!!

T. P. Davis, even though it wasn't all good between us, I still miss your presence. Keep your head up, Big Poppa. Love ya.

To all my fans, what can I say? I love you all. Your love and support means so much to me and I thank you from the bottom of my heart. Enjoy.

Love,
T. N. Baker

|D| |C| |E|

PROLOGUE

"Whose pussy is this?"

"It's yours, daddy!" Enychi would answer me in a soft, seductive tone. "It's yours," she'd repeat, as she slowly rotated her hips, and the walls of her wet pussy squeezed tighter around my dick, causing me to explode all up in it, every time.

"That's right," I'd groan, as I collapsed on top of her sweaty body. The pussy was mine indeed.

WASUAN

Enychi was my wifey for real, and when you talk about a nigga being sprung, I was that nigga fo' sho. Shortly after I met her, I chased her until she finally decided to take a chance on our relationship. I felt I had to lock it down once that happened, so I got her up outta her little shabby-ass apartment, got myself a bigger one, and moved her right on in. I did whatever it took to keep her around me, starting with convincing her to leave them bullshit jobs she had that took up all of her free time and paid a bullshit salary. I understood the fact that baby girl was in college and needed them gigs to pay her tuition, but that was before me. I wanted to be the one taking care of her now. I paid for her education, her hair, her nails, and I kept her wardrobe up with the latest fashion—and rolls of fabric, because most of shorty's outfits she designed herself. Whatever Enychi needed, I got it for her. She had a hard time with that at first, being Miss Independent and all, but I ain't give a fuck, she was my boo, she represented me, so it couldn't be no other way.

In fact, I looked at it as more like an investment, because

shorty was far from being one of them knucklehead chicks with no direction or book smarts.

That's what I loved the most about her, she had goals in life. Graduating from college was very important to Enychi. She wanted to be one of the hottest designers in the fashion industry, so most of her time was spent focusing on school and keeping up with the latest trends, and I supported her 100 percent. I knew that if it ever came down to me needing her, she'd have my back with no hesitation. So the shit I was doing for her wasn't in vain.

Besides, as fast as she could spend my dough, I made it back, jumping in and out of the drug game and shooting dice with some of the gettin'-money niggas on the block. But in the beginning, Enychi damn sure gave me a run for my money with that feisty-ass *I'm an independent woman* attitude of hers. She went hard at playing hard to get, and for a minute there the cat and mouse chase was cute, 'cause a nigga like me always loved a challenge. That is, until all that chasing I was doing seemed hopeless.

But now, everytime I think about her and the two years we shared together, I feel like she was worth every moment of it.

Besides Enychi, that dice shit was another weakness of mine. Just like I loved her, a nigga loved to get his gamble on, too—and I was damn good at it. Fucking with them dice games until all times of the night was how I liked to hustle. Talking greasy and taking niggas' money was what I did. Shit, that was the only thing my pops got to teach me when I was a shorty, before he was murdered. So I had to hold down the legacy. And, that nigga pops was the truth when it came down to shooting some dice. As a matter of fact, one of the many things he said to me about the game was that it was a fast way to make a quick buck or two, and if I was good at it I would never walk the streets broke.

So cats hated to see me hit the block, 'cause if they ain't already have a game going, they knew I was gon' get it started and empty out pockets. I'd start the bank off at no less than a thousand, and by the end of the night the stakes would grow as high as seven grand. On the streets, that was a considerable amount of paper being tossed around.

Niggas couldn't fuck with me. My luck was crazy. I'm not saying I ain't lose every now and then, but that shit was rare—ya heard.

That is, until this nigga named Tone, a light-skinned, gray-eyed, long-braided, good-haired muthafucka, came around and threw a monkey wrench in a nigga's game.

Pretty Tone was an old-school dude. Thirty-five years old and chiseled the fuck up, like all the nigga did was bench-press. He had the words "Murder was the case that they gave me" tatted down his left arm, and a rap sheet, from back in the day, that was crazy. So niggas knew not to let Tone's pretty boy looks cloud their judgment, 'cause dude was still straight-up gangsta.

After serving ten years state time for murder, it's alleged that when the nigga came home he killed his cousin, E-Money, for not honoring the code of the streets. Supposedly, his cousin ratted him out for a murder they both took part in many years ago.

Rumor has it, Tone broke up in E-Money's crib in the middle of the night and slit his throat while he was fucking his own wife, and out of fear for her life she didn't tell the police who had done it.

. . .

Outside of being coldhearted in the streets, Tone wasn't a stupid dude. He served his jail time wisely, by taking advantage of all the educational programs offered to inmates—back when they existed. Then he came home, started a legit business of his own—but on the low, he was still putting in work for his Colombian connect, Pedro. Niggas in the hood knew that clothing store shit was a big front. Still, Tone would come through the block every now and again trying to intimidate dudes by flashing big wads of cash and bragging about his big-boy status. He'd make a nigga so mad that you couldn't help but gamble your last dollar, hoping to roll trips, just to shut his ass the fuck up and take his money, along with the victory. Tone's game wasn't all that nice. It was more the fear he pumped in niggas' hearts that got him over; but his strategy didn't intimidate me one bit.

I remember the first time I met him. I was only thirteen. It was the weekend and the night air was brick. I had just spanked some old head's ass in a game of craps and was on my way into the corner store to buy me a bag of Doritos and juice with my winnings, when these two dudes, parked in front of the bodega in a beamer that looked brand-new, spotted me.

"Yo," the dude on the passenger side called out. "You that young cat niggas is saying got skills with that dice shit, right?"

I looked both men over closely, to see if I recognized them from around the way. Shit, I could never be too careful. Some of these cats thought that, just 'cause I was a li'l nigga they could corner me, strong-arm my little ass, and take all they money back if I won it from 'em. So I had to stay up on mine, all the time. But these cats looked like money, sporting mink jackets and plenty of bling.

"Yeah." I answered with a hesitant nod, after coming to the conclusion that they had to be paid. I never seen them before but I knew the streets was talking about me. One thing I was not was modest. Like my pops, my goal was to be legendary at this, and that's how it was going down. "I'm that dude. Who you?"

"Me? I'm E-Money and this here is my cousin Big Tone." He pointed to the dude in the driver's seat. I looked over at Tone and he gave me a "what up?" nod, which I courteously returned.

"But, yo, check this out," E-Money continued. "Me and some of the fellas is having a gambling party tonight. A little bit of everything is going down—c-lo, some card games, all that shit. I want you to come through. There's a minimum pot of twenty-five hunnid for each game, so maybe we can get this money together, you know, work something out where we both get paid."

"Word," I replied, because them kind of numbers sounded real good, only there was one problem. "Well, I ain't got that kind of bank right now." I rubbed the sides of my pockets trying to play it cool, but in my mind I was thinking, *Whoa! 2,500? That's a lot of money.* I couldn't even front a quarter of that.

"Don't worry about that, shorty," E-Money said. "I'll spot you. But you better be as good as the streets is saying you are."

I stared at E-Money sideways for a minute, as I went over his proposal in my head. Everything that glittered wasn't always gold, and this shit sounded a little too good to be true. *I hope this fool don't think he gon' pimp a nigga, have me doing all the work and he get all the doe.* I thought about it.

Nah, right now is the time to negotiate.

"I'll do it, but only if I can get a percentage on everything I win," I smiled. "I realize you frontin' the money and all, but it's my skills that's gon' take us to the top of the money pile."

E-Money looked over at Tone and then back at me with a smile and nodded his head with approval. "A'ight, I hear that. Young and smart. That's what's up, li'l man."

Tone threw back his head, gave a deep belly laugh, and said, "Yo, you can't be serious, dawg. I know you ain't tryna fuck with this li'l nigga?"

Ingoring that nigga Tone's hateration, E-Money reached through the window on the passenger side and extended his hand. After I stepped up to the car and shook hands with him, he reached into the glove compartment, grabbed a pen and some paper, and jotted down the address to the party. "Here." He handed me the piece of paper. "Just ask for me, E-Money, when you get there, a'ight?" he said as he signaled for Tone to drive off.

I looked down at the paper as the car pulled off, and got excited, thinking, *I'm about to be paid!*

Later that evening, when I walked into the condo, I knew I wasn't dealing with small-time hustlers for sure. Inside, that joint looked like a million bucks. The hardwood floors that welcomed me into the foyer were so shiny I could see my reflection. In the living room, resting in the middle of floor, was a black leather sectional that looked butter soft, and lamps on each table sculptured into different poses of naked women, with a fifty-two-inch, big-screen television posted up against the wall. I had never seen nothing like it before, but for me, it was the vaulted ceilings and marble fireplace that graced the room.

As I took a couple of steps into the mix of things, I noticed the built-in speakers inside the walls that blasted the DJ's latest hip-hop joints. Cats were dripping in gold, platinum, and diamonds, holding stacks of big bills in their hands. Meanwhile, all types of women—Black, White, Asian, some tall, some short, petite, thick, with long hair, short hair, and even weave hair—posted up close to the money-makers, as they sipped on the bubbly.

I couldn't believe my eyes. Just as the shock wore off, nervousness set in. I felt like a fish out of water and there wasn't one familiar face up in there.

"Hey, little nigga, what's up?" said E-Money, as he walked up from behind me, with a cigar dangling in between the left side of his mouth. He circled around me and looked me up and down. "Glad you made it. It's major paper up in here, and these dudes is about it."

"Oh, I see that," I nodded as I continued to examine the room.

"So, you ready to stomp with some big dogs?" he asked as he removed the cigar from his mouth and slightly rolled it between his thumb and index finger. I poked out my chest and answered, "Ready? Man, I was born ready."

E-Money chuckled. "A'ight, that's what I like to hear. But before you dive into that pool of sharks, let's step into my office for a minute. I gotta give you something to get your feet wet with, right?"

He placed his hand around my boney shoulders and led me toward the back bedroom. Outside of the door, he pulled a set of keys from his pocket and proceeded to unlock his bedroom door. Once it was unlocked, he looked up at me.

"One can never be too certain of the company he keeps," he said. "Dem niggas might look like a million bucks, but what millionaire doesn't want another million?" On that note, he stepped aside and allowed me to walk past him into the room.

After closing the door behind us, he walked over to the desk that was part of a white pine bedroom ensemble. Again, he used his key ring to unlock the file console, and pulled out a stack of cash.

"Here," E-Money said, handing me the stack. "That's fifteen thousand dollars right there. Like I said, this some big-dog shit." I stood there flipping through the money.

"You ain't got to double-check my count. It's all there."

"Oh, I trust that," I assured him. I wasn't trying to check his math, I was just fascinated with the amount. I never held that much money in my hand before.

"A'ight now, I'm banking on you, so don't disappoint me." Still rapt in the Benjamins, all I could do was nod my head.

Then, without thinking, I asked, "What you want me to do with all of this money?"

E-Money screwed up his face and answered, "Nigga, I want you to double that shit! That's what I want you to do with it. Hell, you should be able to triple it, if you as good as I heard you were." He threw back his head and laughed, revealing his gold fronts. "Come on, go get up in the game and get your rhythm started," he said as he stuck a fresh cigar in his mouth and led me out of the bedroom, locking the door behind us.

I returned to the main room and lost whatever bit of youthfulness I had. I sipped on champagne and was playing with the best of the big boys. That's when I became a man. Towards the end of the night everyone was gathered around me, the prodigy kid who was getting all of the ballers for their cash and jewelery. One cat even put up the title to his car. The bank had grown to $100,000.

Tone was vexed, and threatened to stop the bank if I continued to play in the game. "Look, I'm callin' it, if that li'l nigga don't cash out," he spat, referring to and turning towards me. "You already done proved you got a big dick, li'l man. So, yo, get up out the game and let somebody else get some of that paper."

"Come on, dawg, stop hatin' on the little dude," said a voice from the back of the crowd.

I was in a zone, as I concentrated on my roll and swayed from side to side to B. I. G. and Method Man's lyrics: "Fuck the world, don't ask me for shit, everything you get, ya gotta work hard for it."

Cool as ice, I commanded the room. I didn't feed into the threatening stares from Tone and some of the cats whose money I'd already pocketed.

I had been playing my best since my first roll that night, and I wasn't doing it for my investor, either. I was playing the game that I loved. For me, dice was more than a pastime, it was more than a hobby or an addiction: It was an art and a gift passed down to me from my pops.

I blew in my hand, shook my wrist, and closed my eyes. I mumbled, "This one's for you, Pop, just like you taught me." I took my time and confidently released the dice.

As the dice hit the floor and froze into position, the room was silent. My gut told me I had it without even looking.

"Trips!" yelled the unofficial game referee. The room went crazy. I was cheered on, as the crowd toasted with bottles of Moët.

"That's what I'm talkin' 'bout! These niggas can't see you, partner!" My cosigner, E-Money, patted my back. "Come on. Let's collect my money." E-Money made my night that night, he put $4,500 in my pocket and, without a doubt, I went home a happy man.

That was twelve years ago, but every time I ran into that nigga Tone, it wasn't hard to tell that he still had a bit of animosity in his heart towards me for making him look bad in front of his people back then.

But, damn, who knew the nigga was out to do me dirty like this . . . I didn't even see it coming.

It's been a minute since Tone rolled them trips and I signed that deal with the Devil, but I remember that shit like it was yesterday.

It was a Saturday morning and I woke up to my dick in Enychi's mouth, as she blessed me with some of her toe-curling head. Baby girl definitely knew how to make a nigga feel good. I must say. I taught her well.

What a way to wake up and start the day!

After she finished sucking the early morning load of man milk out of me, I glanced at the clock: It read 10:45 A.M. I got up out of bed and headed for the shower. I was meeting up with a few of the homies to get an afternoon game of dice going.

By the time I finished washing my ass, Enychi had breakfast waiting for me—grits, cheese eggs, turkey bacon, and some

French toast. Honey went all out. She damn sure knew how to take care of a nigga, and I loved her for that.

"Wasuan, I need five hundred dollars to pay my car note today," Enychi said.

"Oh, so that's why you woke a nigga up like that this morning," I said, referring to her super head job.

"No, I just felt like taking care of my man, that's all."

"Oh, is that what it was?" I laughed, fucking around with her, like I always did.

"Of course, that's what it *is*." She flashed me a devilish grin.

"Yeah, a'ight," I said, wearing a crazy Kool-Aid smile. "Good answer." Yeah, baby girl's morning sweet talk won a nigga over. "A'ight, ma. I'ma have that for you later. Just meet me on the block—a'ight? I'm meeting up with the fellas at about twelve to get my shit off. I might even have a little more than that for you, if niggas come out to play.

"Here, blow on these for me for extra luck," I said, referring to my lucky, iced-out set of dice that hung low from my chain. Enychi nodded her head and walked up to me and gently blew on 'em. "Ain't no stopping me now," I said, as I playfully popped her on that nice, soft, fat ass of hers and sat down to the kitchen table to get my eat on.

"Wasuan, what happens if one day you get in too deep and lose all of our money?" Enychi questioned with a hint of irritation in her tone. "What you gon' do then, huh? Gamble your life away?"

"You crazy. Your man is too nice for that. I stay taking them dudes' money. But if some shit like that was to happen, then I guess my baby, the fly-ass fashion designer gon' have to hold it down for a minute until a nigga bounce back, right?"

"Yeah, but I gotta finish school first."

"True, and that's what you need to stay focused on. Stop worrying about shit like me losing, 'cause it ain't gonna happen, not like you talking. Have some faith in your man, girl. Watch. You'll see!

"One day, I'ma buy us a house, put about four carats on your finger, and pay for one of them fairy-tale weddings—all for you—from the money I be winning from that shit, and *then* I'll retire! Just wait. You'll see. Don't sleep on your man . . . baby girl!"

"Okay, Wa, w-h-a-t-e-v-e-r!" Enychi gave me a 'talk to the hand' gesture as she headed towards the bathroom. "I'll meet you around two—a'ight?"

"A'ight, that's what's up!" I said as I wolfed down my breakfast and headed out the door.

Pulling up on the block, I spotted Mel, Speedy, and that nigga, Durty, posted up in front of the corner store. All three of them niggas was looking beat, like they'd been out slinging them things all night. It was the first of the month, so the fiends copped that get-high all hours of the night, or at least until their money ran out. That's a good look for me, though, if that's the case, because I came to pocket some of that drug money.

These dudes was some funny-ass muthafuckas. Only, Mel was my ace. We grew up together, plotted and schemed together, and even sold drugs together. Difference was, he was good at that shit. Me, I only fucked with it when my money got low, 'cause I realized the drug game wasn't for me once I got locked the fuck up the first time. Moneybags Mel is what niggas called him, because he was getting some serious paper, pushing the kind of product that the streets couldn't get enough of. Mel was about his money, so he didn't fuck around with that gambling shit too hard. When he did, though, it was all good, 'cause he took his losses like a true player; but them niggas, Speedy and Durty, they ain't get them names for nothing.

Speedy was quick to snatch up a few dollars when niggas wasn't paying attention, and Durty, that nigga ain't never play fair. So with them two in the game, you had to watch 'em closely.

"Yo, what up, niggas?" I said, giving each nigga a pound. "What it look like?"

"Ain't shit, Wasuan," answered Speedy. "What up with you, kid?"

"Nothing. Ready to get this dice shit going. What's up? Y'all niggas' pockets is ready—right? 'Cause, yo, I'm ready."

"Hell yeah, nigga," said Durty. "These muthafuckin' pockets stay ready!"

"Yeah, nigga. Well, I hear you talking, but put ya money where ya mouth is!"

"Whatever, nigga." Durty began counting out mad fives and ten-dollar bills. "You ain't said nothing but a word. Bam! That's two hunnid right there—nigga, what!"

Durty threw the crumbled bills onto the pavement like they was on fire.

"Get the fuck out of here, nigga. I came to play. I ain't fuckin' around with no petty cash. But being that it's early and y'all niggas wanna act like a bunch of broke-asses, we could start shit off with five hunnid or better." I laughed, but I was dead up on some serious shit.

Mel threw his five one-hundred-dollar bills to the ground.

"Yo, count me in, dawg. I' ma go in the store and get some dice, 'cause word up, Wasuan. You been on some cocky bullshit ever since you won them last couple of games, but, yo, soon your luck's about to run out. Word up."

"Never that, son," I confidently claimed as he went into the bodega. "Besides, luck ain't had shit to do with nothing—I learned from Pop Wells, the best muthafucka that ever done it. So I couldn't lose!"

The hours passed by quickly and more fellas came out to play. A lot of side bets jumped off, along with a few arguments, 'cause in the hood niggas and money ain't a good mix, and most can't never accept their losses and bow out gracefully.

"Yo, come on, son," yelled cheating-ass Chico, another dude who thought his roll game was tight but always wanted a do-over 'cause of some bullshit technicality. "Run that shit back one more time. It hit my man's shoe!" he said.

"Nah, nigga. Get the fuck outta here! That roll was straight, dawg. How many times you gon' run shit back? You aced out, you cheatin-ass muthafucka!" I picked up the dice and put them to that nigga's mouth. "Here blow on these, nigga," I joked, as Chico cut his eyes at me and knocked my hand away.

"I'm about to kill it, a'ight . . . uhhhh," I said, tossing the dice to the pavement. "Trips, muthafuckas. *What!* Pick up ya face and pay up—damn, y'all niggas ain't tired of me taking y'all money yet?" I teased just to get them niggas more agitated than they already was.

"I'm ready to play for real now. I got ten Gs. What's up? Come on. Scared money don't make money. My pops taught me that!" I laughed as I challenged the crowd of about fifteen niggas standing around, but they ain't want it wit' me. Just as I was about to get into a bunch of shit-talking and name-calling on those scared, frontin'-ass niggas, I heard Enychi call my name.

15

"Excuse me," Enychi said as she fought to get past all the gawking-ass niggas admiring her fine ass. She was sporting a denim mini skirt. "Excuse me," she repeated again, "Can I get by, please?"

Finally she reached me. "Hey, baby," she said, kissing me softly on my lips before she continued. "You got that for me or what?"

I took her by the hand and walked her back towards her car to get her out of the faces of them thirsty-ass niggas.

"Yo, where's the rest of your skirt at? Didn't I tell you I was gon' have that for you? Here. Here's fifteen hunnid, now go buy yourself some fucking pants. I'll see you later on, when I get home." I kissed her lips quickly and rushed her off.

"Okay, baby, thanks," Enychi said, not ashamed to count the money in front of me to make sure it was all there. Once it was confirmed, she had a smile on her face that could light up a room, then she hopped back in the candy apple–red Dodge Viper that I copped for her and sped off.

"Yo, how the fuck you pull her, nigga—she bad!" Chico threw back his head and laughed.

"What, nigga! Yo, dude, stop sweating mines and put some real fuckin' money up so we can get a real dice game going!"

"Yo, word. Wassup, Wasuan?" Tone rubbed his chin. "Shorty, do look mad good! Is that wifey, or just some chick you jumping off with?"

"Nigga, that's wifey, so wipe the muthafuckin' drool from ya mouth, all y'all thirsty-ass niggas, and let's roll some fucking dice!"

"A'ight, cool." Tone nodded his head. "Ten Gs you said. That's it? Come on, player. That's what you call real money, dawg? I blow that shit on shopping for my girl's shoes, my man!"

"A'ight, then. Whatever, nigga! We could get right. How much you talking?"

"Oh, I know I could get right, but you sure you wanna fuck with me? 'Cause I know you ain't ballin' like that, dawg."

"Yo, dawg. What, you tryna play me? You don't know how the fuck I'm rolling, so don't play me—play these muthafuckin' dice. Matter fact, call the bet." Tone was acting like he really had it in for me, so I had to bark on his ass.

"A'ight, yo. I'ma call it. Fifty grand off the top from me if you win, and vice versa if I win. Plus an extra ten until one of us rolls trips," he said.

I almost choked when Tone threw them kind of figures at me. I should've known something was up, but my love for the game was too strong to doubt myself or let a nigga see me sweat. I wasn't running no matter how crazy the numbers was, I came to play and was there to win that shit.

"Oh, you switching up the rules like that—cool!" I said in a skeptical tone. "I ain't got that much on me now, but if I have to, which I doubt, I'll have my girl go in the stash and bring that to you."

"Yeah. Well, get ready to have her fine ass do that. Your roll, nigga!" Tone responded sarcastically.

I was shitting bricks, I ain't gon' lie. My heart was pounding like a muthafucka. Just then, Mel walked up to me and grabbed me by my arm. "Yo, dawg, don't fuck with that," he said.

"Mel, chill, I got this."

"Nah, man, you in over your head with this one." Mel had a concerned look on his face.

"Yo, you gon' roll, nigga, or what?" Tone interfered.

17

"Yeah, I got this, dawg." I snatched my arm from Mel, shook up the dice a little longer then usual, then tossed them to the ground like they were balls of fire burning up the inside of my hand.

"*Umm!*" I released the dice and as I leaned in close to see what I had rolled, Mel walked off, shaking his head with an irritated look on his mug. "*Damn!*" I yelled, disappointed as hell when I looked down and saw 1, 6, and 5 on the face of them dice.

"Yeah, nigga. That's ten big ones to go with that fifty! You can handle sixty, right, Small time?" Tone threw back his head and laughed. Then he held out his palm. "Be ready to pay me mines, dawg. Word up, I got this. Bam!" He rolled, but it wasn't trips either.

"Yeah, a'ight, you yellow muthafucka! I'm 'bout to show you that light skin went out of style a long time ago. What we fucking with now, seventy? Okay—okay, now that's what I'm talking about, real money, nigga."

Tone rubbed his chin but didn't say anything.

I kept on talking shit just to get under his skin. "You sure you ain't ready to quit now, you clown-ass muthafucka? That's right, 'cause this right here is a grown man's game. I'm about to put a big dent in your pockets, dawg." I twisted my mouth to the side, then added for emphasis, "For real."

I continued to talk shit 'cause that's what I do; but on the real, nobody ever had me under pressure like this. Then again, the stakes never been this high before. Hell, I felt like I was going to see my parole officer with dirty urine on a day I knew she might ask for samples. That's how nervous this nigga had me.

I wanted to win so bad, my palms was sweaty and my dick was hard. *I gotta win this*, I kept telling myself.

Come on, baby, come on. I pleaded as I said a silent prayer to my pops and hoped that he heard me. *Please let these be trips, Pops!* I kissed the lucky dice around my neck before tossing the ones in my hand.

I tossed the dice and looked to see what fell. "Shit! Still no good." I rolled a 2, 4, and a 5.

Tone stepped up to the plate. "A'ight, dawg. It's over for you. I'm done fooling with your punk ass. No more talk. Bam! Yeah, nigga. What! That's eighty big ones. Give it up!"

Tone let out a whooping war cry, as the crowd, roaring with excitement, started to jump around in celebration of his victory.

I just stood there shaking my head in disbelief as I looked down at the dice that read the numbers 6, 6, 6.

Ain't this a bitch, three sixes—the sign of the fuckin' Devil.

Tone was real hyped up and doing a lot of bragging and boasting, talking more shit than a little bit, as he stepped to me and said, "Yo, you ain't call that pretty bitch of yours yet? Come on, dawg. Get on your horn. Call her up and tell her to crack open your piggy bank."

"Yo, I see you got jokes. You got that, though. Just chill with all that, dawg. I'ma call her when I get ready to." I was trying to buy myself a little more time to figure out how I was gon' break the news to this nigga, 'cause I ain't have that kind of cash for this cat.

"What? Come on, dawg. You tryna play me now? I ain't waiting for mines. Bad enough I gotta wait for your broad to bring it to me." Tone started to get a little hostile.

My hands was still sweating like a muthafucka, and the niggas that stood around started to clown the shit out of me, saying stuff like: "You need a loan, dukes?" and, "Yeah, nigga. I thought you couldn't lose—where's all that loose shit-talk at now, player!"

I heard it all. Niggas was real reckless with the mouths, coming at me sideways with all their foul-ass comments. I had to think fast, though. I ain't wanna tell the nigga I ain't have it in front of everybody. I pretended I was dialing Enychi, which gave me the opportunity to ease away from the crowd noises. I was ready to make a run for it. No lie.

Only, that nigga Tone was definitely keeping his eye on me. "Yo, man, don't go too far," he said, watching me hard, like a panther ready to pounce.

This nigga was really bugging the fuck out, but then again, eighty Gs was a lot of damn loot. Shit, even if I sold some drugs to come up with that kind of money, it still would take me more than a few nights on them street corners.

Speaking of corners, my boy Mel came to mind. *I could just get it from him easy, and give it back later, or put in some work*, I thought. But, nah, I eased off that notion quick. I knew Mel; he ain't mind looking out for a nigga when I needed it, but he wasn't too keen on tossin' around his paper for nonsense. And blowing money like that on some gambling shit was definitely foolish to him. Not to mention the fact that he tried to stop me, so for sure I knew he was gon' be on some ol' *I-should-of-listened* bullshit.

"Fuck it." I ain't have no choice but to be a man about the situation and let that nigga know what the deal was. "Yo, let me holla at you for a minute," I said, signaling Tone to join me where I was standing.

"Here we go with the bullshit," Tone said as he walked towards me.

"Check this out, yo. I only got half of the eighty right now, but I can have the other half to you in about two week or so."

Tone shook his head no. "Yo, dukes, is you trying to play me or something? Nah, dawg. You talk big, so get me my money. I want all my cash, now."

"Well, I ain't gon' be able to do it then. If I ain't got it, then how I'ma give it?"

"A'ight then. I guess it ain't nothing else to talk about." Tone's voice remained calm as he pulled out his Glock and pointed that shit in my face. I tensed up. Staring into the barrel of that gun triggered a painful memory of mine.

I remembered the gambling spot, the clouds of cigarette smoke, and the loud voices from the spectators that whooped and hollered as they watched the game of craps. I was only ten back then, but I studied my pops's style hard every time he rolled, and I would watch them dice clash and tumble to the floor, relentlessly revealing winning numbers.

"Yeah, Pops," I cheered him on because I was proud of my old man.

Suddenly, one of the angry players, jumped in my pops's face. "Hell, nah, ma'fucker. Fuck that. You cheating, nigga! Them dice gotta be loaded." The riled-up gambler was a dude named Gunz, a big-time hustler who was a known for starting shit. My pops told em, "Ah, go'n wit that bullshit. I got skillz, nigga. I ain't gotta cheat." I knew that was the truth, 'cause outside of his ability to roll them dice the way he did, my pops taught me to always play fair. He believed in the honor of the game, and despised a cheatin'-ass nigga.

I could hear their dispute getting heated, but as a shorty, I couldn't see what was going on, once the towering crowd began to gather around to watch, as scrams beefed with my pops. Then suddenly, in a matter of seconds, I found myself standing in the middle of chaos—loud screams, and the thundering rush of feet that followed the sound of gunshots that rang out.

As the smoke cleared, I realized that my pops had been hit. I watched him drop to his knees in slow motion, clinching his wounded chest as blood seeped through his fingers. The painful look I saw in his eyes broke me down. He struggled to speak his last words to me. "I love you, son," he said—and just like that, right in front of my eyes, the only nigga I ever loved was gone, robbed of his life over a fuckin' dice game, and there wasn't shit I could do about it!

My heart raced and sweat dripped from my forehead, as the memory of my father's murder forced me to understand that this Tone shit wasn't a game; it was for real. Once I came to terms with that, the bitch came up out of me. I started copping all kinds of pleas. Fuck it, I didn't care. My life was on the line.

"Come on, Pretty Tone, man," I called out to him, hoping that the sound of that would soften his killer instincts. "Why we gotta take it there? I'ma pay you, dawg. My girl gon' bring you forty now, and I'ma give you the rest by the end of next week, man. Just give me 'til next Saturday—that's my word on everything I love. Come on, dawg. Don't go out like that over no forty grand." I started dialing Enychi for real this time, 'cause dude didn't look like he was tryna hear nothing I was saying.

"Yo, 'Nychi. You home? Good! I need you to look in the top

drawer on my side of the bed and get that key—it's to my safe. Open it and bring me the money that's inside of it, I'm on the block, a'ight? Hurry up!" I slammed down the hood of my cell phone before she could start hitting me with all types of questions. Besides, I ain't have the time to be explaining nothing to nobody.

After I made the call, Tone tucked his gun back in the waist of his jeans. "Yo, if this was back in the days, you would have been scattered all over this fucking sidewalk by now. I'ma work with you, though, but I'ma need some type collateral for that."

"Ah, man, thanks. Anything. Yo, here, take my chain. It's worth about ten Gs, and the diamonds on this shit is official." As soon I took it off and tried to convince the nigga that the chain was valuable, Enychi pulled up. A nigga like me was relieved and happy to see her, like never before.

"Yo, man," Tone said, "put your chain back on." His eyes focused in on my chick like she was fillet mignon and the nigga ain't had a good meal in weeks. "I want something that means more to you than that fucking chain. I want her, right there," he said, licking his lips.

"My girl?" My voice cracked. "Get the fuck outta here. What kind of shit is that?" This nigga was really trying to play me like my name was Willie Lump-Lump or something. *What the fuck is he on? Some fuckin' indecent proposal–type shit?*

Tone pointed at Enychi with his noticeably warped finger. "Yeah, her right there. I wanna fuck the shit outta her, and you could even watch if you want, but I promise you I'ma put a hurting on her pretty brown ass." He laughed. "And your punk ass might not be able to handle that, Small Time."

"Come on, dawg. You real funny, yo! How you wanna bang

my girl out? Matter of fact, how the fuck you expect me to ask her to do some bullshit like that? She ain't gon' do no shit like that in the first place!"

"I don't really give a fuck how you tell her to do it," he said, with a blank look on his face that said it all. "Tell her your life's on the line, and I guarantee you she'll go for that."

"Wait a minute. You gotta be kiddin' me." I needed some further understanding from that dude. "Are you saying, if I let you fuck my girl, we even?"

"Nah, nigga, I'm saying, by me fucking your bitch—that buys you a little more time to pay me the rest of my paper. That's all." Tone gave me a *duh—you dumb muthafucka* expression.

"Yo, come on, Tone, that shit ain't making no kind of sense to me," I said, angry.

"It don't have to, nigga. But that's what it is unless you can pay me all my shit now, or take that bullet."

I wasn't no bang-bang, shoot-'em-up kind of dude, but I swear, I was ready to kill this muthafucka. This shit had to be deeper than a dice game, because he was really trying to do me dirty. That shit didn't sit well with me at all. I was at a hard point. *Should I call this nigga's bluff or go along with this twisted shit?* I contemplated for as long as I could, and no matter how I looked at the situation, either way this nigga Tone had me by the balls. I looked over at my baby as she sat in her car with the motor still running, her lips poking out with attitude all over that pretty face of hers. *Nah, I can't do that to her, so fuck it!* "Yo, man, do what you gotta do," I blurted out.

"A'ight!" Tone said, in a *be more than happy to* kind of manner, as he did some type of hand motion and two rugged-ass niggas walked up on me, holding their T-shirts up so I could see the metal that was tucked in the waistline of their jeans.

"Yo, ya'll niggas know what it is," Tone said, with authority behind it. As those dudes move in on me, I knew it was about to go down, and, since Mel wasn't around to go to bat with me, I folded. "Wait, man, a'ight! I'ma talk to her, yo." I wasn't ready to die, not like this, so what other choice did I have?

I walked over to Enychi's car feeling like a straight sucker as I opened the passenger's side door and got in. I didn't know how the hell I was gon' ask my baby to do some bullshit like that.

"Wa, how much money is this? I mean, this is ridiculous, is that all your money? Wasuan—you need some fucking help, boy!" Enychi went off on me instantly as she threw the plastic bag filled with money in my lap. Shaking her head, she sucked her teeth in disgust. "I can't believe you," she mumbled.

"You right, ma. I can't believe it either, and I agree, I do need some fuckin' help. I know this shit's crazy." *I ain't never fucking around with them dice after this shit*, I said to myself.

"Whatevah, Wasuan. Just get out my car, please, 'cause you say that, but I know your fucking ass gon' be out here all night trying to win that money back."

"Nah, wait a minute," I said, taking a deep breath, 'cause I ain't even tell her the other half of it, and I could see Enychi was already fed up with my bullshit.

"I'm listening," she answered with a nasty attitude.

"A'ight. You was right when you said I need some help and I'ma get that, I promise. You do know that I love you to death, right, baby girl?"

Enychi pursed her lips. "Yeah, I hear you," she answered in a *whatevah, nigga* type of tone.

Damn, she was making this shit harder for me than it already was, but I continued.

"Enychi, I need you to do something for me, not 'cause I want you to—'cause, believe me, I don't—but I need you to do this for me because you love me."

"Wasuan, what the fuck are you talking about?" Slightly raising her voice, Enychi looked at me and rolled her eyes. "I know you ain't coming at me with some more bullshit," she said.

"Just listen, a'ight? This shit ain't easy for me, right here. I owe this nigga dough that I ain't got right now, so he's bugging the fuck out." As I carried on, Enychi huffed and puffed, which was a clear sign of her frustration.

I paused for a moment. This wasn't easy for me at all. "Baby, you see that light-skinned muthafucka standing over there?" With a discreet nod of the head, I pointed Tone out to her. Tone was staring back at both of us, a smug look was written all over his face. Damn, I wished death on his ass right then and there for this. I wanted to tell Enychi to just drive off, but instead I took a deep breath and blurted it right out to her. "I need you to sleep with that dude for me, or it's lights out for ya man. He's gon' murder my black ass."

"You need me to what? Oh, hell no!" she snapped. "Wasuan, how much fucking money do you owe that guy?"

"All together?" I mumbled. "Eighty grand, and this right here is only half of that."

"Eighty thousand dollars!" she yelled. "Oh, you are so gone. Wasuan, I told you your fucking gambling habits was gon' get you in some shit—now, look at you! You gon' try to fucking pimp me to settle your fuckin' debts! What the fuck is that about?"

Enychi's arms were waving all over the car as her voice got

louder. "What kind of shit is that to ask me? What am I? Your bottom bitch now—I'm not your girl anymore?" She frowned up her face as if she had just tasted the bitterness of something sour.

"You a foul-ass nigga for even asking me some shit like that, you know that?"

"Enychi, come on, ma. You think I wanna have another muthafucka running up in you? You know that's some bullshit?"

"Then why ask me to, Wasuan?" Enychi sounded like she was fighting back tears.

I didn't even know how to respond to her question, so instead I just flipped the blame on her. "I just told you why, what the fuck! You the one that jinxed me in the first place, talking all that shit this morning about me losin', and then you bring your fuckin' ass up here in some little short-ass skirt, talkin' 'bout 'excuse me,' just enticing muthafuckas, the way you swished the fuck past 'em. That's probably why the nigga really wanna fuck you now!"

"Oh, so you tryna say this bullshit is my fault?" Enychi yelled.

"Nah, you know what? It ain't; and you right. I shouldn't even had brought this shit to you. I fucked up, so I'll deal with the consequences.

"Fuck it. Just let this nigga do what he gotta do and get it over with. As long as you know that I love you with all my heart and I always will, I'm cool going out knowing that." I hit her with the guilt trip, kissed her on her cheek, and started to make my exit from her ride.

"Wa—wait. You forgetting your money." Enychi's watery eyes started to slowly release one tear after another.

"Nah, I ain't forget it. You keep it. If this nigga gone kill me regardless, I might as well die owing his ass the whole 80 Gs, right?" Enychi's response was delayed as she stared out her windshield like she was battling her thoughts.

"No, wait a minute, Wasuan." Enychi reached out and placed her hand on my shoulder. "I'll do it. Go tell him I'll do it."

And right then I swore I'd never get caught out there like this again.

ENYCHI

I love Wasuan. I can't even front about it. He's every-thing to me. When we first got together our relationship took off in full speed. When we weren't with each other we were on the phone, especially after nine o'clock, free talk time. I had been on a strict budget at the time, so I had to monitor my min-utes. Wasuan would come over and chill with me for a couple of hours after I got off work; but since my place was so small and I had a roommate, he never spent the night. I got off of work kind of late, but some nights I'd sleep over at his apartment, although sleeping was the last thing we did. We'd make love, watch TV, talk, and spend the rest of the night making love some more.

Needless to say, I never made it to class on time in the mornings. Which wasn't like me to do, but I was falling in love. Wasuan quickly became my lover and best friend, and on our one-month anniversary, when he asked me to quit my jobs and move in with him, I said yes. I wasn't too sure about quitting my jobs at first, but he convinced me. And, I must say, since Wasuan came into my life two years ago and forced me to depend on him, life for me has been so much easier.

I say forced, because at first it was hard for me to accept anything from him, or any man for that matter, especially money. I had always vowed to myself—after growing up and watching my mother degrade herself, using one man after the other for financial gain—that I would never follow in her footsteps.

What made it even worse was she calls herself a Christian. True, she never missed a day of Sunday service, or Thursday-night prayer and worship, but I learned early on that, just because you attend church regularly, that don't make you a Christian. You see, mommy dearest preyed on the pastors, deacons, and ministers of large congregations. It would start off with her volunteering for one of the many church programs. Then she'd find a reason to set up a one-on-one meeting with the house's leader. Next, she'd be getting a hands-on healing of her own, along with some of the money from church collections to take home with her. Funny thing is, her disreputable behavior wasn't a secret, but she always managed to get one of them fake-ass church figures entangled in her web of lustful sin.

Her motto was, "The larger the following, the bigger the collection of tithes and offerings." And, yes, through the years she maintained a very comfortable lifestyle for us, while her men kept her in the finest jewels, a variety of fur coats, classy Sunday dresses, with handmade hats to match, luxury cars to drive—not to mention giving her access to their churches' cash. She kept me in the finest designer fashions, name-brand shoes, and private schools. I don't know what it is she does to those men, but she has to be good at it.

The last time we spoke, she was leaving the dealership in her new Benz. That's how my mother rolls, only in the best. I ain't saying she's a gold digger, but she damn sure knows how to milk a cow. She works her game. And now she's working it on her new husband, Reverend Burns, in their beautiful, new, six-bedroom house in Norfolk, Virginia, where she lives now. I have no idea what her obsession is with church figures, but I always hated it. Attending church regularly as a child, I discovered that that's where all the gossipers, liars, cheaters, and sinners were.

Every Sunday during Sunday school, I was mistreated by the teachers, who were of course the wives of some of those no-good, cheating hypocrites. Not one was fit to be called a man of Christ.

Lord knows, I've tried hard not to be my mother's child—not literally, because I loved my mother and respected her for providing the best for me. And even though proper morals wasn't something that she exhibited herself, she still made it her business to instill them in me.

"Enychi," she would say, each and every time she was dumped by another one of them so-called men of God, "when you grow up, be your own woman, okay, honey? Don't ever put yourself in a position where you need a man to take care of you. Go to college and get your education; be independent so you can hold your head up high when you're driving in your fancy car and living in a big ol' house that you paid for. I didn't get past the tenth grade, and shortly after I got pregnant with you. Your father . . ." she'd pause for a moment, then continue, "that's another story. But him and his family didn't want nothing to do with us, and when my mother found out I was expecting she threw me out the house." She'd laugh—but it was one of those laughs to keep from crying. "I've never looked back. I wanted to keep my baby, and that's what I did. So, I do what

I gotta to do for us to eat and live the way we do. You get what I'm saying, don't you?"

"Yes, Mother," I would nod. At fourteen years old, what was I supposed to say? "Stop sleeping around and get a job?" I don't think so!

After I graduated from high school, my mother told me it was time to stand on my own two feet. The next thing I knew she had picked up and moved to Virginia without notice. I was stunned at first, and then fear set in. I had no real family that I knew of to turn to for help. I had no idea what I was going to do in order to survive.

Becoming a fashion designer had been my only dream for as long as I could remember, so for me there was no plan B. I was going to go to college to major in fashion design no matter what.

I ended up enrolling in college and applying for financial aid. With financial aid covering only half of my tuition, I managed to hold it down working part-time as a waitress at Red Lobster, a cashier at Macy's, and a cashier at Foot Locker, all at once, without a dime from my mother. And then Wasuan came along.

I hate to be cliché, but they say the apple doesn't fall too far from the tree, and I fell from the same tree and into the same world of dependency that I had watched my mother live in.

Although my mother probably doesn't remember the names of all of the men she's been with, let alone claims to have loved, I can truly say, from the bottom of my heart, that I am in love with Wasuan. It's never been about what he could do for me or what I could do for him in return. That's the difference between my mother and me. That, right there, will always be the difference.

Once I graduate at the end of the year from F. I. T., the Fashion Institute of Technology, I plan to take the fashion world by storm, so I can hold my man down like he does for me. I've always told Wasuan I would do anything for him, except rob, steal or kill without cause, so I guess it was time to honor my word. But to sleep with another man over a dice game gone bad was just plain ridiculous.

I couldn't understand how he could ask me to do something like that. I knew Wasuan loved me, but I also knew he loved to gamble. Now, I questioned which one he loved the most.

As he walked away, Wasuan beckoned for Tone to come over to my car. While Wasuan went over to the crowd of guys standing around, probably to gamble some more, he didn't even look back at me. I was so pissed at him, he had me feeling less than a woman; but at the same time I felt sorry for him, because I knew that Wasuan had a problem with gambling and I had done nothing to help him get help.

Meanwhile, Tone walked over to my driver's side window. "What's up, beautiful?" he said as he held out his hand to introduce himself.

I gave a fake smile, but didn't extend my hand to meet his.

"You want my arm to fall off?" Tone said, trying to come at me with some ol' wannabe smooth Billy Dee Williams weak-ass line.

I rolled my eyes at him hard, 'cause I wasn't the lady singing the blues, and he damn sure was no Billy Dee.

"A'ight," Tone said, as if he got offended by my look. "I know this is no doubt an awkward situation for you, but once you get to know me, you might fall in love."

Ahh, who did this Terrence Howard look-alike, trying-too-hard-to-be-charming nigga wit braids think he was?

Not only was he humiliating the shit out me and my punk-ass man, but the tired-ass rap he was tryin' to run was killing me. He couldn't be serious, so I didn't even entertain his silliness. *How could Wasuan let him do this to me?* I said to myself as I cut my eyes at Tone again. "Yo, let's skip the small talk, my man. How we gon' do this?" I said as I mustered up every ounce of aggression that I had up in me.

He laughed and said, "Whoa, chill, ma. Don't be like that. I'ma treat you like the lady you are—a little wining and dining first, a'ight? Meet up with me tonight around ten, if that's cool?"

I let out a hard sigh and said yes, but, to be honest, I had no intention on spoon-feeding this nigga. Although it seemed like he had other plans, I wasn't tryna ration out my time; if I had to fuck him I wanted to do just that and be done with his thuggish ass. He handed me his number on a business card that read "Big Tone's Urban Wear, Street Fashion for the Gangsta in You" and told me to give him a call at about 9:30, so he can tell me where to meet him at.

I studied the card before I stuck it in my purse and even gave him a few cool points for having his own business. That is, if the card was official. After I agreed to the arrangements, I started up my car and, before pulling off, I took a quick look around to see if I saw Wasuan, but I didn't. When I got home he wasn't there, either. I ran straight to the house phone and tried calling him a few times, but my calls kept going straight to voice mail. It was six o'clock then. By the time eight rolled around, he still wasn't home, nor was he answering his phone.

I had anger building up on top of anger. I couldn't believe he had the audacity to get us both in this mess, and now he couldn't even be man enough to come home and face his fuck up. My first thought was to not even go through with it. God knew I didn't want to; but how would I ever forgive myself if something were to happen to Wasuan? I gave up on trying to contact his trifling ass though, and headed for the shower.

After allowing the hot water to massage my body for a good twenty minutes, I massaged myself with some Cherry Blossom body cream, from Bath and Body Works, then I sprayed a few squirts of Be Delicious perfume by DKNY on my neck, belly, and private part. I'm a lingerie type of girl, so I had a drawful of sexy garments to choose from. I decided on my hot pink, lace Simone Perele panties and matching bra. As I put them on, I took a look at myself in the full-length mirror. "It's like candy," I sang out loud. *Hell, I might be the talk of the town after a stunt like this; but one thing that nigga won't be able to say is that I didn't look and smell damn good!*

When I finished getting dressed it was already a quarter past nine. I was so nervous, but I knew I had to go through with this. I tried not to think about it too hard.

Grabbing my car keys, purse, and Tone's business card, I left the apartment. As I sat inside my car and listened to the radio to kill time, Mario's song, "How Could You?" came on the radio, and the lyrics stirred up my emotions all over again.

. . .

I thought back to the first time I met Wasuan. I gave him nothing but attitude every time we bumped heads. Eventually, I think his patience started to wear thin, because all of a sudden, whenever we ran into each other and I was with my girl Denita, he'd speak to her and ignore me. Strange but true: Him not paying me any attention is what made me realize I liked him. Thinking of Wasuan, I tried calling him one more time, but once again my call went unanswered. I flipped the phone closed, furious.

I had no idea where I was meeting Tone at, so before dialing him I had to get my head together about what was about to go down. I took a deep breath.

Time seemed to be moving extremely fast; the clock on the radio read 9:27. I took another deep breath, hoping that it continued to move just as fast throughout the night. I pulled my cell phone from my bag and proceeded to dial Tone's number.

On the second ring Tone picked up. "A'ight. Punctual. I like that in a woman."

"Oh, yeah," I said dryly. "Well, just remember, I'm not doing this 'cause I want to. So where do you want us to meet up at?"

"I'm not far from you, so why don't I just come scoop you up?" Tone suggested.

"How do you know where I live?" My curiosity was piqued.

"Come on, ma. This is my 'hood. Ain't too much I don't know or can't find out. You in Rochdale, right? Circle One?"

"Yeah."

"A'ight, then. Come downstairs."

"I'm one step ahead of you," I said as I got out of my parked car and waited close to the curb.

"That's what's up? I'm coming around now."

I heard a loud *vroom-vroom* sound, as I looked towards the entrance of my circle and spotted Tone wearing a shiny black helmet, quickly approaching me on a Suzuki Hayabusa motorcycle. He slowed down in front of me and my thoughts escaped out my mouth. "You can't be serious. I ain't getting on that thing."

Tone lifted his helmet, wearing a big grin on his pretty-boy face. "Ahh, don't tell me you afraid?" he challenged me.

"Afraid? I'm not afraid! I just didn't know that's how you was rolling," I lied. Truth be told, it usually turned me on to watch a man ride a motor bike, but I was scared as hell to partake in the ride.

"A'ight," Tone said. "Here's your helmet. Hop on then."

I hesitated. Finally, I put the helmet on and fastened it, then straddled myself across the big, black, polished bike, wrapped my arms tightly around his waist, squeezed my eyes shut, and prepared for takeoff. The motorcycle roared when Tone revved up the engine for the ride.

The wind blew mildly as we zipped in and out of traffic at a fast but not intimidating speed, and, unexpectedly, it excited me. We reached the Greenwich Village section of Manhattan in fifteen minutes, and in three more we were in front of a dimly lit Caribbean restaurant called Negrils.

I gazed around and had to admit the restaurant's setting was a very romantic one. As the hostess seated us, a soulful mix of R & B jazz graced the air while the candlelight from each table flickered just the right amount of radiance off the walls. As we were being seated, Tone stood up and waited until I was seated before he sat down. I was surprised, but I didn't let on that I was impressed by his manner.

Immediately after being seated, the waiter came over to our table with the menus and took our drink orders. Mine was a Guava Mimosa, while Tone ordered a bottle of Pinot Grigio for himself.

"Have you ever tried Pinot Grigio?" Tone asked.

"No, I'm not much of a wine drinker."

"Well that's too bad, because it goes pretty good with Caribbean food."

"This is a really nice spot," I said a bit reluctantly.

"Yeah, it's cool. Is this your first time here?"

"Uh-huh."

"Well, I'm sure you've been to places much nicer than this."

I cracked a phony smile. I knew that was his way of indirectly trying to find out whether or not I've been exposed to nice places before now. I wasn't about to admit to dude that Wasuan and I hadn't been someplace really nice in a minute.

Just in time, the server came back with our drinks and was ready to take our food order. I ordered the black bean soup for an appetizer, followed by the jerk shrimp and plantains, and Tone ordered a salad, the escovich fish, and rice and beans.

The restaurant was somewhat crowded, and I could see why. Not only did the food smell good, it tasted delicious. Throughout dinner I didn't say much. I didn't like Tone at all, and my attitude toward him obviously expressed that. I kept thinking that in any minute my man was gonna barge up in there, stand his ground, and claim what was rightfully his. I checked my cell phone constantly to make sure it was on, and that I didn't by any chance miss Wasuan's call. But I guess him calling was just as unlikely as him walking up in there. Wasuan not trying to contact me only made me angrier, and being angry only made me drink more. Two glasses of wine on top of cheap champagne had me feeling more than buzzed, so I was geared up and ready to seal the deal. Only, Tone wasn't ready yet.

After he paid for dinner he suggested we check out the restaurant's lounge on the lower level. Tone carefully held onto me as we walked down the steps. I guess he noticed I was a little tipsy. Downstairs, the art deco ambiance was just as chic as the upstairs, only the scene was a bit more intimate, and from the looks of it, the small crowd of people seemed to be enjoying themselves, the music, and of course the drinks from the bar. Ironically, the DJ was spinning Maxwell's lyrics, "Maybe you might be more than just a one-night lady," from his Embrya CD.

We sat down in the only available spot next to the DJ and his turntables. As if on cue, the waitress rushed over and Tone ordered another bottle of wine. It was by surprise that I found that I was actually enjoying myself; but, sadly, it made me realize what I was missing out on, because, although I loved Wasuan, he never took the time to take me anywhere anymore. I mean, sure he laced me with nice things, but he never laced me with his time.

In the beginning of our relationship, Wasuan had gone out of his way to make me happy. We took trips, ate out at fancy restaurants, and he even ran my bathwater. Now his idea of a good time is boning me until I'm sore, giving me money, and watching the latest movies on bootleg DVDs together. What's funny is, up until tonight I was cool with that. I guess you never miss a good thing until you're confronted with what you've been missing.

"So, what do you do for a living?" Tone asked.

"I'm in my last year of college, and once I graduate I wanna start my own clothing line for women."

"Okay, that's what's up. I see we got something in common." Tone smiled.

"Oh really, what's that?" I said as I took a sip of wine.

"Well, I got a degree in business management and I own a clothing store; and you're about to get your degree and you're interested in designing clothes. So, who knows? Maybe one day I'll be selling your designs in my store."

"No offense, but I'm gonna design classy clothing, not urban."

"Come on, ma, I ain't offended. Classy is what's up. Besides, every thug needs a lady, right?" Tone said as he cracked another smile.

I frowned up my face. "So what college did *you* go to?"

"Prison State University." Tone laughed. "Nah, but seriously, I got my degree while I was locked up."

"Locked up? What'd you do, kill somebody?" My sarcasm slipped out.

"Nah, but that's what I was accused of."

"Wow. I'm sorry to hear that." I was trying hard to ignore the fact that I *began* to find Tone attractive, and for some reason his hooligan disposition made him even more interesting.

"It's all good! Thanks for the sympathy, though." Tone briefly brushed his hand across my thigh. "So tell me some more about you and that classy line of yours."

Before I knew it, Tone and I were engaged in conversation like two people out on a first date, interested in getting to know one another. I shared quite a few of my fashion ideas with him, and while he was busy being impressed by them I turned off my cell phone, assuming if Wa was going to call, he would of done so by now.

"Do you dance?" Tone asked out of nowhere.

"Huh?" I replied, caught off guard.

"Dance. You know, like this," he stood up and did the coolest little two-step.

Damn, and he's got a sense of humor, too, I thought. "Yeah, I do a little sumthin'-sumthin', but I don't see no dance floor."

"It's all good. We can make one," he said as he held his hand out for mine. "Come on, let me see what you workin' wit."

I tried to hide the smile that was creeping across my lips. "Why not?" I said, as I got up and followed his lead as we created own little dance floor. We worked it out real smooth to Luther Vandross's "Excuse Me, Miss" and then picked up the pace for Mary's "Family Affair."

"Damn, you're gorgeous," Tone said as he stared into my eyes while doing Fat Joe's version of the lean-back dance.

I started blushing like a bashful little schoolgirl with butter-flies in her belly.

"If you was mines, I would've just gave up my chain or whatever else I had to give, because I couldn't have shared you with anybody." He paused in midsentence, took another look at me, and continued. "Nah, I couldn't do that," he repeated as if he had just thought it over with himself.

I stopped dancing and stared at him. *Was he insinuating that Wasuan's lucky chain was an option, and he chose to give me up instead? That can't be!* Nothing in this world would have convinced me to believe that. My mood had just been spoiled by his lies, but I had to ask, "Were you really gonna kill him?"

Tone looked confused. "Kill 'im? Come on, now. Do I look like a killer to you?" Innocently smiling before putting on a straight face, he continued. "Nah, seriously, I did a lot of time in jail over some nonsense, and I ain't tryna go back over no bullshit. Why, is that what he told you?"

"Just forget it; it's getting late anyway. Let's not prolong tonight's intentions any longer." I was so bothered that once again I was seconds away from reneging on the deal.

"Whoa, my bad, ma. I ain't mean to upset you."

Yes, you did, I thought. Tone wasn't stupid and neither was I. "Don't worry about it," I said instead. "It ain't like we're on a real date or anything; this is an arrangement, right? So let's just get out of here, go do what we gotta do, and get it over with, okay?"

"A'ight," Tone said blankly as he signaled for the waitress to come over with the check.

This time, with no hesitation I hopped on the back of his bike. As he zoomed through the city's streets, I couldn't help but bury my head into his back and tightly clutch his waist. The wine must've enhanced a few of my senses, because the night air felt like it was blowing straight through me. I could also smell Tone's cologne. He was wearing 212 for Men by Carolina Herrera. I shook my head. That's one of my favorites. I had purchased it for Wasuan, but he was kind of stuck on his Jean Paul Gaultier, so he never wore it. For my own pleasure, I'd spray our bed sheets with it every now and then, and that worked for me.

Not only did Tone smell good, his tight body felt damn good as well. He was so buff, like he worked out on the regular and took care of himself, which was another thing Wasuan didn't do. Even though he was tall and skinny, he still needed to get in somebody's gym just to get fit.

I realized I was doing a lot of comparing.

What is that about? I had to check myself, because Wasuan was my man. I loved him, no matter how mad I was at him right now. It had to be the alcohol that had my mind going like this. I was only doing this because he asked me to. Which made me angry all over again, because he should have loved me enough not to put me in this situation. I knew I loved Wasuan, but at this very moment I felt like I hated him just as much.

Tone pulled up to a motel in Queens. "Wait here," he said as he got off the bike and walked through the motel's revolving doors. Minutes later, he emerged with a smile and told me our room was on the first floor, located on the outside. We found an open parking spot directly in front of the room door.

The moment we entered the room, Tone led me straight to the bed and got down to business. He started by removing my clothes.

"Wait a minute, what are you doing?" I asked as I pulled away from him.

He stood in front of me with a confused look on his face. "What you mean? You said you wanted to hurry up and get it over with, right?" Tone looked me up and down as he continued, "Yo, I'm just trying to do what you asked me to do."

"Okay, but I can take my own clothes off," I said in an unpleasant tone, as I sat down on the end of the bed and slowly started to remove my black pumps.

"Yo, I'm sorry if I pissed you off, but, umm, you can keep them on," he said as he kneeled down in front of me and slipped the heel of my foot back in my shoe. "Damn, you're so damn sexy." Tone slid his hands up my knee-length skirt and with eager strokes, he gently caressed my thighs.

I tried to fight it, but the way he was massaging my legs started to relax me, and before I knew it I was laying back on the bed.

"You like that, don't you?" Tone whispered as he rubbed his fingers across my panties. I almost panicked when I felt how wet I had gotten. I questioned whether it was the alcohol making his touch feel so good to me, or was he just that fucking good. Immediately, I lifted up my blouse and Tone took the initiative to unfasten the small gold clasp on the front of my bra. Gently he bit down on my nipple while he massaged my breast, and chills shot through my body like shock waves. Right then and there, I knew he had skills.

Kissing me softly but with conviction, the rhythmic flow of his tongue was intoxicating and a little intimidating. I was so overwhelmed, I kept my eyes closed and refused to think about how messed up this situation was. As Tone pulled me closer, I couldn't help but wonder if his tongue could French-kiss my pussy the same way.

Stopping abruptly, Tone got up off of me and demanded, "Take them clothes off. I'll be right back." He then grabbed the empty bucket from the dresser and went out the room. I undressed slowly and laid back down on the bed, covering my quivering body with the comforter as I nervously awaited his return. I was about to give myself to a man I didn't know, love, or even like, and that was scary.

Minutes later Tone came back with a bucketful of ice cubes. Seemingly excited about what was about to go down, he began to quickly undress. And I can't lie, I carefully checked out every inch of his six-foot, four-inch muscular frame as he removed each piece of clothing. His medium-size, hard dick bounced and bobbed up and down as he stepped out of his Polo teddy bear boxers. Wasuan had him beat in the size department, because Wa was hung like a horse when he *wasn't* hard.

Still, I couldn't ignore the fact that Tone was fine—so fine I almost climaxed from the sight of him, and I was mad at my hormones for giving way to a stranger so willingly. He walked over to the bed, kneeled down over me, and started licking my neck. Gliding his tongue down towards my stomach tickled me lightly, as some parts of my body caught chills and other parts got all hot, bothered, and moist. I couldn't believe that I was responding to another man's touch this way. Slowly separating my legs, Tone began to insert ice inside of me, and instantly my hot box turned each cube into liquid. As the water trickled from the lips of my pussy, he gently thrust his fingers in and out of me, pushing them deeper and deeper. The excitement took control of me, as I bit down on my lip and aggressively gyrated my hips in circular motions. I lifted my waist up from the bed to greet Tone's wide tongue, as he ran it across my wet opening. He slid his hands under my trembling thighs.

Softly moaning, I grabbed the back of his head and bathed his face with my juices, until my clit started to pulsate.

I closed my eyes and welcomed this never-before moment of pleasure. My entire body began to shudder as I climaxed.

"Ahh." I let out a sure sigh of satisfaction.

Amazed by this sexual pleasure, I couldn't have uttered a word if I'd wanted to. Tone finally came up for air, wearing my juices all over his face. I had great sex with Wasuan, but his foreplay never felt this good. I rolled on my side into a fetal position and I tried to get ahold of myself, as my pussy still throbbed to a rhythm of arousal. And from the way Tone hopped up from the bed with that smug look on his face, I knew he wasn't done with me yet. Walking towards the full-length window, Tone pulled back the curtains and placed the chair in front of it. "Sexy, c'm'ere," he called out.

I eased myself off the bed to go to him. At first my knees buckled, I felt so weak.

"Hold onto the top of this chair and bend over for me," he commanded.

I look at him and then out of the window, "What if somebody sees us?"

"That's what makes it exciting. Come on, just try it, a'ight?"

I hesistated for a moment before mounting the chair, and as soon as I did Tone got behind me and started rubbing his dick on my ass. This was some weird shit to me, and it sure as hell wasn't something I was used to. I was scared that someone was going to see us, but as Tone plunged his dick inside of my wet pussy, lust overpowered my resistance.

"Umm," I moaned, pushing out my ass to savor every inch of his hardness.

I kind of went with the flow until a couple walking past took notice and started to stare. I was uncomfortable. This wasn't my idea of being a lady at all. Noticing me tensing up, Tone whispered, "Relax," as his sensual thrusting slowly became ferocious strokes.

Wasuan, I'ma kill you for this!, I thought to myself, as I closed my eyes and let go. I began to perform for that couple like I was a porn star, making contorted facial expressions, while I screamed out sexual obscenities. Obviously, Tone was getting too excited by my overexaggerated act, because he started to pound faster and harder, as he growled, "Raargh! Gimme that pussy!" As wet, sloshing, slapping sounds rang out loudly, Tone spoke aggressively. "Tell me you're daddy's little whore," he said, smacking me on my ass.

He threw me off with that kind of talk. I didn't know how to respond to it, so I didn't answer at all.

Pop, pop, pop. Tone spanked my ass three more times, causing it to sting, as he demanded, "Let me hear you say it!"

"Yes, I'm daddy's little whore," I yelled out in a pitch that said satisfaction.

"Damn—work that pussy, bitch! Work it! Yeah, just like that—don't stop."

"Aaa-aagh-aah," I cried out increasingly louder, holding my mouth wide open, as he fucked me faster, and faster, and harder.

"Do that shit, ma! I'm 'bout to cum. Ahh—yeah, right there—right there!" Tone inserted his finger into my mouth and I sucked on it like a baby would a pacifier. Suddenly, his body started to jolt while his sweat dripped on my ass, and I could feel the heat from his cum as it flooded my insides. Fulfilled and exhausted, Tone shut the curtains and together we dropped onto the bed. Tone wrapped his arm tight around my waist and started snoring no sooner than his face hit the pillow. I had every intention of getting up and going home right after I got a few moments of rest, but reluctantly I fell asleep.

By the time I woke up, the sun was rising. I eased out of bed, put on my clothes in a hurry, and left without saying good-bye. I stood in front of the motel feeling like a cheap whore after what had happened. As I waited for a taxi, I turned my cell phone on to see if I had any messages. To my surprise I had twenty-five. The first five were from a very apologetic Wasuan, expressing how much he loved me and how he felt like less of a man for putting me through this.

Fifteen voice mails later, he was all over the place, placing all the blame on me, saying things like we set him up, it was over between us, I must have wanted it, how could I let a another nigga fuck me, and how, if I really loved him, I would have been answering his calls.

This boy has really gone bananas. I told myself not to trip over this, 'cause, for one, Wasuan wasn't a drinker, but from the way his words slurred, I could tell he might have had one too many. And two, even though I still can't believe I enjoyed everything about last night, it was over with, and I just wanted to put it behind me.

My cab pulled up, and as I opened the door and sat down in the backseat, I could feel Tone's cum oozing out of me. *Damn, I played myself.* I hadn't asked him to use a condom. Pregnancy was the least of my worries, because I was on birth control, but thoughts of contracting a sexually transmitted disease scared the shit out of me. How could I have been so stupid? The last thing I needed was for Wasuan to find out I let Tone run up in me unprotected.

It was a little too late to start thinking smart after the fact, so I said a little "Please, God, don't let me have nothing" prayer, just to be on the safe side.

Fifteen minutes later the taxi dropped me off in front of my building, and as soon as I opened the door to our apartment I spotted Wasuan passed out on the couch, with two empty pint bottles of Hennessy lying on the floor beside him. My first instinct was to go over to him and slap the shit out his face. But for what? I just had the best sex ever. Besides, not only was it six in the morning, but the situation was so awkward that facing him was something I didn't look forward to, so I wasn't gonna wake him.

I eased past him and headed straight for the bathroom, as Tone's sperm continued to leak out of me. I had to sit in some hot water and soak myself. Stripping off all of my clothes, I threw them into a trash bag. I knew if I ever wore them again, it would only remind me of the night I spent with Tone, and I didn't want that to happen. As I scrubbed the sweaty sex from my body and douched Tone's cum from my pussy, my emotions swung back and forth from anger to guilt. I couldn't help but to sit in the water for a few moments longer just to analyze my relationship with Wasuan. *Will it ever be the same after this? I know if he doesn't quit gambling, it's over for sure!*

Finally forcing myself up out of the bathtub, feeling worn out, I headed straight for the bedroom and fell back to sleep.

Later that morning I opened my eyes and sighed with relief, realizing that it was all a nightmare. Not sex with Tone, because unfortunately that did happen, but I had dreamt that in the middle of my sexcapade with Tone, Wasuan had come into the motel room and, together, they had taken turns fucking me like wild animals in heat.

"Wasuan!" I yelled, before I got up out of bed and walked into the living room to see if he was still sleeping. But to my surprise he was already gone. I can't say that him just leaving, without us discussing what had happened last night, didn't leave an ill taste in my mouth, because it did. I went into my purse and pulled out my cell phone so I could call up my best friend, Denita, just to get her take on the situation. I knew she would tell it like it was without any sugar coating.

Denita and I met during our freshmen year of college. We're complete opposites. She's light-skinned, I'm dark; she wears her hair in microbraids all the time, and I wear mines in a wrap; she's the feisty one, while I'm more reserved. But for some reason, we just clicked and been joined by the hip ever since.

"What up, girl?" Denita answered on the first ring, which was normal. That girl's phone was like her Siamese twin, they were joined by the ear. She was so scared she'd miss something—anything—if she missed a call.

"Hey, 'Nita," I responded, with a hint of frustration.

"Uh-uh, girl, why you sound like that?" Denita said, instantly picking up on my attitude.

"Girl, you don't wanna know."

"Sweetie, um, this is Denita you're talking to, and you know I always wanna know! So what's up, girl? Come on, spit it out."

"A'ight, but I'm only telling you this 'cause you're my girl—because it's kind of embarrassing."

"What, girl! *What?* You're killing me."

"Okay, okay! Do you know this guy name Tone, who owns a clothing store on Jamaica Avenue?"

"He light-skin, with pretty hair and nice eyes?" Denita asked.

"Yeah."

"His store's on 165th Street, across from the Coliseum, and he be riding on a black Suzuki bike, right?"

"Yeah, but, damn, girl, don't be knowing the nigga's four-one-one like that!"

"And, why not? That nigga is *fine!* I don't know him personally, but my brother does, so what about him?"

"Ahh, I fucked him last night."

"What! Wait a minute, did I hear you right?"

"Yes, I had sex with him!"

"Bitch! What, you gotta be lying. Enychi, are you serious?"

"Yep!"

"What? How the fuck did that go down, what happened with you and Wasuan? You and that nigga's like Will and Jada, Beyoncé and Jigga, Mary and whatshisface? Anyway, fuck all that! Just tell me what happened? Did y'all break up or something?"

"Girl, no, we did not break up! But here's the funny part, Wasuan is the one who asked me to do it."

"Get the fuck outta here, you can't be serious? Why would he ask you to do some dumb shit like that?" The initial excitement in Denita's tone turned to disgust.

"I don't know, something about Wasuan owing Tone some money that he don't have, so Tone threatened his life and then told him if I sleep with him he'd let him live."

"That's fucked up. Who does that? Does my brother know about this?"

"I don't know, but he wasn't out there when I pulled up with Wasuan's money."

"How much money was it?"

"Girl, he had me go in his safe and empty out forty thousand dollars."

"Forty Gs!"

"That's what I said, but get this, he owe Tone eighty! Fucking with those damn dice."

"Enychi, you know your man got a problem, right?"

"Yeah, I know; but what can I do about it?"

"After asking you to do some shit like that, I'd leave his ass alone. I mean, how could he just let a nigga straight herb him like that? What did he say when you came home?"

"That's the thing. When I was calling him last night he wouldn't answer, and when I woke up he was already gone. It's like he's ducking me!"

"Yo, you should leave his ass! I would've told him to kiss my ass, and left his ass right then and there."

" 'Nita, what was I supposed to do? Say no—and then, if something happen to him, feel guilty about it for the rest of my life?"

"No, blame that nigga for taking bets his ass ain't got the bank to cash-in!"

"Come on, 'Nita. So you're telling me, as open as you are off of Rodney, if he asked you to do something like that for him, you wouldn't?"

"Hell, no—and no offense, boo-boo—but Rodney's pistol-toting, box cutter–carrying, thug ass ain't gon' first let a nigga come at him like that!"

"Whatever, Denita. If he asked you, you would."

"Okay, believe that bullshit if you want to. I'm not even gonna sit here and argue with you about it."

"Who's arguing? All I'm saying is, you mean to tell me you could ride in a car with that nigga for five hours, when you know he's driving dirty, and risk your freedom, but you won't sleep with another dude if he asked you to? Come on 'Nita, tell that to someone that don't know you like I know you."

"No, you come on! I rode with Rodney because I wanted to.

D I C E

He ain't ask me to, and we're taking about something totally different, like that nigga's respect for you. Where is it? You know what, don't even answer that. You did what you felt was right, so who am I to judge you? You still my girl!" She let out a sigh and said sarcastically, "So since you did fuck Tone's fine ass, at least let a bitch know his MO in the bedroom. Is he straight gangsta in the sheets, like he is in the streets?"

I smiled, sank down in the sofa, licked my lips, and prepared myself to tell Denita every detail about my night spent with Tone.

I broke out early this morning to avoid bumping heads with Enychi. Last night had me all fucked up, so facing her wasn't something I was ready for. What fucked it up even more was she spent all night with that nigga Tone, and all I kept thinking about was how he was out somewhere fuckin' my girl, and still expected me to pay his ass the rest of that money. That alone should've broke us even. I had to make moves, but knew I was gon' be the comedy for the day on the block, so before I subjected myself to the bullshit, I put my pride to the side and called up my boy Mel.

"Aye, what up my nigga?"

"Ain't shit. How you?" Mel asked, as if he was a little concerned.

"Man, I'm fucked up all around the board right now," I admitted.

"Yeah, I heard you took an L last night, fuckin' with that nigga Tone."

"Ahh, man, that nigga did me dirty, kid!"

"Man, I know how Tone get down, that's why I tried to tell

you don't fuck with that nigga. He real dirty wit his shit. But what happened? Did him and homegirl get up?"

"I guess so. I wasn't at the crib when she left, and she ain't bring her ass in until this morning."

"Yo, Wasuan, man, you my nigga and the whole nine, but how you let some shit like that go down with your girl, dawg?"

"Come on man, dudes was running up on me with guns and shit, what was I supposed to do? You bounced on a nigga!"

"Hold up dawg, you making it sound like I left you for dead, and that ain't even how ya boy get down. On the real though, when it come to tossing them fuckin' dice around, you don't know when enough is enough, and that shit ain't cool, my man."

"Well, fuck it, that shit is water under the bridge now." I ain't wanna hear that shit Mel was talking, but what I did wanna know was, what could he do to help a nigga out. "But, yo, you got forty grand I could borrow?"

"Nah, not right now, all my doe is tied up. I could probably help you out with some of that in a couple of days, but you gon' have to put in some work for me though."

"I got you, but, yo, I'm on my way to the block to see if I could get my money up with this little grand I got in my pocket, a'ight? I'll holla at you later."

"No doubt!" Mel said.

Around my way, I knew I could get dudes for at least three or four grand in no time, but I had to get my head right before I could fuck with them niggas. I hit up my man Jamaican Jack for a fat twenty sac of what he called "that yard weed," got me a Dutch, and sparked myself a nice size blunt. Now I was game.

As soon as I hit the block, I saw the little dudes posted up on each corner on the lookout for the boys in blue, so I knew the fellas had to have a serious game of dice already popping right in front of the neighborhood's favorite bodega. I parked the Impala, and as I walked up niggas started laughing out loud and shit, tryna clown me, but I kept face. My mind was on getting money. I was high, my confidence was strong, and I felt that after losing my dignity last night, I ain't have shit else to lose.

Without even asking what the bank was, I said, "Yo, I got the ends on what's left in it."

That's when these foul-ass dudes really tried to come at me crazy. I was hearing it all. The nigga Durty was singing, "If that's your girlfriend, she wasn't last night."

Chico's hating ass was holding the bank, so he was on some, "Yo, the bank is a thousand strong. If you lose, nigga, I got next, a'ight? Not on the roll. I'm talking 'bout wit' that fine-ass broad of yours, n-i-g-g-a!"

He didn't know it yet, but he had it coming to him for that slick ass comment. I disregarded all of the disrespect long enough to get my count up. My anger was my motivation. I hit c-low on my first roll, which brought my pockets up to 2 Gs.

"Yo, fuck you, nigga!" Chico yelled. "Stop the bank!"

"Whatever, dawg. My bank is two thousand. Ya'll niggas know the rules. Trips pay double." I prepared for my next roll. I threw the dice and landed a 1, 2, and 3, which should have meant I aced out—but since one of the dice was leaning from a crack in the pavement and couldn't be stacked, I got to run it back. I caught trips my next roll, quadrupled my dough, and walked away with the bank, since niggas ain't wanna put up no

more doe. Before I broke out, I walked over to Chico and
punched him in his punk-ass mouth. I was tight about that
fucked-up shit he'd said earlier, and I had to gain some respect
from somebody, so why not start wit that nigga?

"Have next on that, *bitch!*" I said as I walked over to my car,
grilling everyone of them niggas, waiting for one of them to say
something else crazy. I got in my ride and sped off. I was thirty-
four grand away from getting out of Tone's debt; but there had
to be another way, 'cause I was gonna start making enemies real
fast, if dudes kept up the disrespect.

When I walked in the crib, Enychi was in the living room,
on the couch, watching "Flavor of Love" on VH1.

"Hey, how you?" I spoke nonchalantly as I walk past her to
the bedroom.

"Wasuan, we need to talk," Enychi said, as she got up and
walked up to the door of our bedroom.

"What? Right now?"

"Yeah, right now. What's up with you? Why do I feel like
you're avoiding me? I called you a million times last night and
you wouldn't even answer your phone."

"Well, I did call you back," I answered in an irritated tone.
"A bunch of times," I added.

"Yeah, after the fact. But I'm talking about before I even
left the house." From her approach, I could tell that Enychi was
just as angry with me as I was with her.

"So, was the nigga good?" I had to ask because the curiosity
was killing me.

Enychi looked at me like she wanted to slap my face.
"What? I'm not gonna answer that! It's bad enough you pimped
me like I was some fucking trick, now you wanna sit here and

harass me about whether or not I enjoyed being pimped? Come on, Wasuan, focus on why I did it instead!" she yelled.

I knew why she did it, but for some sense of security, I needed to hear her say she didn't get any pleasure out doing it, so I asked her again, "Enychi, I already know why you did it; but did you like it?"

"Wasuan, you are un-fuckin'-believable," Enychi said, still avoiding the question. She shook her head and stared at me like every ounce of her respect for me as a man had just left the building.

"You know what? I'll be whatever you want me to be, but I ain't stupid. I saw the way you looked at that nigga Tone when I pointed him out to you. You was feeling dude. You had to be. You stayed out with him all fucking night. I wouldn't be surprised if y'all set me up."

"You're insane. And where do you get off thinking you can blame me for your bullshit? This was your fuck up! I wasn't the one out there shootin' them fucking dice around like I ain't have shit to lose. That was you! You put the price tag on my body. So don't stand here and act like you lost your fucking memory; you know why I slept with that man! And it wasn't because I liked him or was attracted to him. I didn't even know him, for God's sake, never saw him before in my life until yesterday, and you know it. The only reason I did it was to save your ass, you fucking ingrate, and don't you forget that!"

"Ooh, 'ingrate,' so that's what I am now?" I asked, just for the sake of sarcasm.

"Among other things," Enychi slyly responded, with her neck rolling and her arms folded.

"Huh—well, it's good to know that all the paper I spend on

your tuition ain't going to waste, smart-ass." I felt I had to remind her of some of the shit I've done for her as well.

Enychi's expression turned cold. If there was one thing I knew
she hated, it was having something that I've done for her thrown
up in her face, so I knew I'd hit a nerve with that comment—and
that was my intention. But I felt bad after I said it.

"Damn, baby, I'm sorry. I ain't mean that. It ain't even you
I'm mad at. I'm the one that's tripping. I just feel fucked up, like
I ain't even a man for letting that shit go down—that's all. I
should've tried to kill that nigga with his own fuckin' gun."

"Wasuan, what's done is done. We can't change it, so let's
just forget about Tone and this whole fucked-up situation, okay?
Can we please just go back to it being about you and me?" Enychi walked over to me and wrapped her arms around my neck. "I
love you and only you, Wasuan Jameek Wells," she said, address-
ing me by my full government.

"I love you too, Enychi Michelle Carter." I hugged her back,
kissing her lips passionately as I started to undress her. I wanted
her badly. Enychi was gonna be my wife one day, so when the
foul images of Tone and her together popped in my head, I tried
my best to keep in mind that she had done it for me.

ENYCHI

From that night on there was nothing but trouble on the home front. The harmony in our relationship shot straight to hell. Wasuan couldn't seem to find it in his heart to put what happened with me and Tone behind him. It was like he looked at me totally different. Even his voice had the sound of disgrace in it when he spoke to me, and the high level of respect that he use to have for me was obviously fading. Wasuan was punishing me for doing something he had asked me to do, and he knew he was wrong for that. He never thought to ask me how I felt about doing it, or would I do it? The nigga straight came out and said *I need you to sleep with that guy over there, and if you love me you'll do it!* I've played the scenario over and over again in my mind, and I know I should've said no, but I guess I'm a fool for letting my heart do the talking, huh?

Lately, just to avoid an argument with Wasuan, after class I'd hang out with Denita or go to the public library. I spent a lot of my time at the library sketching my designs and gathering as much information as I could about fashion, the industry, and what it took to be a designer and run a business. One day, I'm

gonna stomp with top dogs like Roberto Cavalli, Donatella Ver-
sace, Valentino, David Meister, Kay Unger, and so on. I have to.
It's been my dream, since I was a litte girl, to see supermodel
Naomi Campbell strutting down the runway in my designs, and
I was determined to make that happen.

Today, Denita and I headed over to the gym, like we always do
every Wednesday after class, to get our cardio workout on.
While we were on the treadmill, Denita started going on and on
about her mess of a man, Rodney.

"Girl, I'm seriously thinking about leaving Rodney's no
good ass alone for good this time."

I didn't respond, because if I had a dollar for every time I
heard her say that, I swear I'd be rich. On top of that, 'Nita was
quick to give out advice, but sometimes I felt she needed to take
heed to some of it herself.

"You hear me, girl? Enychi, what's wrong with you, because
you've been acting funny all day? What, you and Wasuan still
beefing? I told you, you should just leave his sorry ass. I'm sure
his dumb ass thinks about you and Tone every time he looks at
you now. So it ain't gon' work, and I know he gotta be feeling
real stupid for that move he made."

Denita was right: Wasuan sure as hell had me stressed out;
but I didn't want to talk about it, so I directed the conversation
back to her. "So, what did Rodney do this time?"

"Girl, let me tell you," Denita said as she sucked her teeth.
"Remember, I told you he was supposed to go out of town to
handle some business?"

"Yeah?"

"Well, how come, when I was in the cab going to the train station this morning, I called his cell phone and some bitch answered, talking 'bout Rodney's her man and they been together for two months?"

"What did you say?"

"I ain't get to say nothing, because as I was about to cuss her ass out, I heard Rodney's trifling ass say 'What I tell you about answering my phone?' And then the line went dead. Now the nigga won't pick up when I call."

"Well, 'Nita, you've been messing with Rodney for how many years now? Five, right? And according to you all he does is cheat on you—and you ain't leave his doggish ass yet?"

"I know; but when the dick is good, it ain't that easy."

"Well, let's just hope his good dick don't get you sick, girl."

"Oh, hell no! I make his ass wear a rubber every time I give him some of this pussy. But wait 'til his ass come home thinking he gon' get some. I'ma stab his black ass, that's what I'ma do."

" 'Nita, you talking crazy right now; that nigga ain't even worth it. All y'all do is fight over the lies you catch him in and the bitches he done slept with, so why you wasting your time? You should've been moved on and left *his* no good, gang-banging, ho ass alone."

"I know, girl. I need to leave Rodney's tired ass alone and you need to leave Wasuan punk ass alone; and when we blow up, them niggas is gon' be so sick!" Denita laughed and held up her hand for a high five.

"Girl, I know that's right!" I smiled, as our hands collided.

WASUAN

As the days slowly passed, my situation with Enychi went from bad to worse. Every time I wanted to make love to her my dick wouldn't get hard. I questioned her a lot about that nigga Tone. I wanted to know if his shit was bigger than mine, was his sex better, and whether or not she liked being with him. I couldn't help it. Whenever I looked at her, I thought about her sexing that nigga. I pictured her giving the pussy to him the same way she gave it to me. I fucked up big time for this one, and I never felt so much regret for anything I had ever done.

Still, I was trying hard to get the money up to settle my debt, and that had me stressing the fuck out, too. I had a couple of days left to scrape up the rest of Tone's money, but I had to put that dice shit to the side for a minute, because it was too much of a win-or-lose situation, and since I had a lot on the brain, my game was a little off.

Mel knew I wasn't good at selling that crack shit hand to hand on no corners, so he set me up behind the scenes. All I had to do was cook, cut, and bag up the shit for him at his mom's crib, and then his street teams handled the rest. On top of giving me some work, he looked out and came through with ten grand to go with the ten I already had, and then he offered to flip the twenty grand into a better profit—although he expressed over and over again how disappointed he was with me for letting Tone play me out like that, and Tone still expecting payment. He said, since I opted to go out like that, his mind was telling him stay out of it, but I was like a brother to him, so he had to look out. I couldn't have been mad at him if he chose not to help a nigga out, because Mel held me down during my first bid, not to mention that when I came home; he put money in my pocket, gave me a place to stay, and while I was on parole he hooked me up with bogus employment, paperwork, and pay stubs to keep that P.O. bitch, Ms. Williams, off my back. So I was more than grateful to that nigga. But I can't front. I was happy as hell he decided to help me up outta this shit.

Finally, I could relax a little, knowing that this money situation with Tone was almost under wraps. I got even more 'laxed once dudes chilled out with all the jokes and when the gossip finally started dying down on the streets. My routine didn't change much. I was still hanging out on the block, but I only fucked around with that dice shit lightly. I noticed Tone would often zoom back and forth through the block on his bike, and that made me feel like the nigga was trying to intimidate me, because he ain't never rolled through the block like that before. We locked eyes a few times and Tone wore this smirk on his face that said, "Yeah, pussy, I fucked your bitch; and no, I don't respect you."

The thought of murdering that dude crossed my mind many times, but body-bagging a nigga just wasn't in my heart. I took my frustrations out on Enychi more and more, though.

No matter how hard I tried to let it go, my insecurities still managed to move full speed ahead. I had to know Enychi's whereabouts, and I watched her like a hawk when I could. I turned into a jealous nigga, all up in her shit. I didn't trust her. I'd check her cell phone, her purse, and even her panties, to see if there was even a hint of sex or a latex scent in them. And, of course, I still loved her; but our relationship had become so distant, I didn't know how to fix it.

ENYCHI

Wasuan was driving me up a fucking wall. Ever since I slept with Tone, our sexual endeavors have been replaced by limp-dick disaster, and when I'd try to make a move on him he'd push me away. I felt like he wasn't attracted to me anymore, and that started to tear down my self-esteem even more. Eventually, enough was enough. I couldn't stand the rejection or the fighting that was going on between us any longer. Every time we tried to sit down and address the situation like adults we ended up in a shouting match, so our level of communication was all fucked up. It was obvious that our relationship was coming to an end, and while I was fighting to salvage what little was left, Tone was calling my cell phone several times a day, filling my voice mail with sweet messages that I ignored.

That is, until an argument about me wanting to go to a movie with Denita got out of hand, because Wasuan went into one of his jealousy fits. It wasn't the first time an argument blew up about me going out somewhere, but it was the first time Wasuan had spoken to me in such a vile manner. I could handle being called a bitch because I've been called that before, but when he had the audacity to call me a slut, that's when I was ready to boil a nice big pot of hot water and throw it in his face. The sad thing is, I loved him too much to leave him, but I was fed up. I started sleeping on the sofa and stopped speaking to him altogether. Since he wasn't bringing any positive energy to our relationship, then why should I?

Two days after the big fight between us, I was on my way to my early morning class when Tone rang my cell phone. I looked at his number as it posted on the screen of my cell and the state of my relationship with Wasuan crossed my mind—so I answered. "Hello?"

"Ahh, hello. Enychi?" Tone sounded like he was surprised that I had actually picked up instead of my voice mail.

"Yes, who is this, and how can I help you?" I asked, as if I wasn't familiar with his voice.

"You can help me by seeing me again."

"Excuse me! Who is this?" I continued to play it off.

Tone sucked his teeth. "Come on now, you know who this is, yo. It's Tone."

"Oh, what's up? It's kind of early to be calling people, don't you think?"

"Nah, I don't. Not when I've already called and left numerous messages on people's phone in the afternoon and at night, and can't reach 'em and they don't return calls."

"Well, why are you trying to reach me anyway?" I knew the answer to that question, but I wanted to hear him say it. Besides, at least somebody wanted to feed my ego.

"Come on, ma. You know why. I wanted to see you again, that's why."

"Well I'm sorry, but I can't!" I guess I didn't realize how

bothered I was with everything that had been going on between me and Wasuan until that very moment, because out of nowhere I broke down and started to cry.

"Yo, ma, you a'ight?" Tone's voice grew concerned.

Sniffling, I searched my car for tissue. "Yes, I'm good," I answered in a firm tone, suddenly feeling embarrassed.

"Yo, you don't sound like it."

"For real, I'm okay. It's that time of the month, so sometimes I get a little emotional for no reason at all. That's all."

"Yeah, I hear you," Tone said, but the way he said it sounded like he wasn't buying what I was selling.

"So, when can I see you? It ain't gotta be nothing like before. I just wanna see you. Maybe grab some dinner or meet up for lunch, or even breakfast, you know? Something like that."

I thought about it for a few moments. *You know what, why the hell not?* was the conclusion I came to. Wasuan wasn't giving up any type of affection, and Lord knows I needed some. And I was already being accused of cheating, so I might as well cheat. "All right, my last class is over at twelve noon. We could do lunch, if that's okay."

"What? Anything you say is okay. Can you meet me on Park Avenue South?"

"Sure can."

"A'ight, then, cool! Have a good day in class, ma!"

I met up with Tone after class at a restaurant called City Crab. It had only been two weeks since me and him slept together, but all of the nonsense that Wasuan had been putting me through made it seem like months. We sat at our table, placed our orders, ate, once the food came to the table, and talked for about two hours.

After I left Tone I couldn't stop thinking about him. It wasn't my intention to start sleeping with him, but he showed interest, gave me the attention I was needing, and we were drama-free, unlike my situation at home. So I started seeing him every chance I could. It wasn't easy, with Wasuan keeping tabs on me the way he did, but when a woman really wants something, she finds a way to get around the obstacles that stand in her way. In the beginning, my plan was to sleep with Tone maybe one or two more times and then ask him to squash the other forty thousand as a favor to me. Assuming that he would, I felt that Wasuan and I could move on and be happy again. Call it strange, but, more than anything, I wanted my relationship with Wasuan to work, because, although we were going through it, I was still in love with him.

Sad but true, Wasuan was still spending a lot of his time out in the streets doing what he does the best, I suppose. Only, now he called me every thirty minutes to check up on me. On occasions I was somewhere bent over in a doggy-style position, getting pounded out by Tone, who does what any nigga would do that knew the rules of the cheater's game. He'd slow it down and fucks me quietly until I get Wasuan off the phone.

The only time I could really get away for a few hours without Wasuan constantly calling me is during the hours I had class. So, quite a lot of times, instead of doing class I was doing Tone. Tone and I would meet up at different hotels, or sometimes he'd pick me up from school just to hang out.

Our relationship was based on sex. For me, sexing him was exhilarating. But outside of bumping and grinding, we also spent a lot of time talking, sharing thoughts, goals, and each other's plans for the future. Basically, we were just enjoying the moment, or so I thought.

"You know, I'm really feeling you, right?" Tone stared at me as I was putting my clothes back on after another one of our hot and steamy sessions.

"Oh really? Well, I'm feeling you, too." I smiled at him.

"Nah, I mean, I want you to leave that nigga and be with me, *a real man.*"

I was caught off guard with that one, because sure I enjoyed screwing Tone, and I even liked his company, but I loved Wasuan. I may not like him right now, but I wasn't ready to be without him. Not for Tone, not for anybody.

"Look Tone, I like what we have, but it's not that easy for me to just up and leave, so can we please not complicate this any more than it already is?" I said, playing it as safe as I possibly could.

"Yeah, a'ight." Tone didn't sound too pleased with my response and barely kissed me back as we parted.

WASUAN

I was on my way home, and in good spirits for the first time in what seemed like forever. Not only did Mel flip my doe, he tripled it, and on top of that I was making a nice piece of change with the business arrangement we had going. Shit was finally starting to come together for me. My confidence was rising, money was flowing, and I even chilled out on gambling altogether. Now I could finally hit Tone's faggot ass off with that forty grand and put this shit behind me.

But first I had to make shit right between me and my baby again. We'd been beefing with each other for way too long, and I was tired of that shit. All this shit was my fault to begin with, the arguing, too. We went from being crazy in love to just plain crazy in a fuckin' month. When we weren't fighting there was the silence treatment, and when I slept in the bedroom Enychi slept on the couch.

So, it was definitely time to get all this Tone nonsense out the way, before I ended up losing my world. I rushed home, ready to take Enychi in my arms and tell her how sorry I was for everything I had put her through. I wanted to look in them beautiful eyes of hers, so she could see the sincerity in mine when I told her how much I loved her, needed her, and wanted to spend my life with her. I had my whole apology word for word memorized, but once I got to the crib Enychi was already knocked out, sleeping. I looked at the clock, it was only nine o'clock. Laying down behind her I wrapped my arm around her waist. "Nych, you sleeping?" I whispered in her ear, but Enychi didn't answer.

When I woke up in the morning, Enychi was already gone, I thought. Until I got up to go to the bathroom and saw the door closed. Before I could knock, I heard her laugh. I leaned up against the door and listened. I ain't know who she was talking to, but she was on the phone making plans to meet with some-body. All I heard her say was she was leaving the house now, so just meet her there in thirty minutes. I ain't know where "there" was, but I sure hoped like hell that was Denita she was talking to.

As I followed less than fifty feet behind her, Enychi entered the parking lot near her school. I slowed down and pulled my Im-pala to the side of the curb and watched long enough to see her park her car and go into the school building. Satisfied with see-ing her walk inside, I pulled off. Strangely, as I reached the sec-ond traffic light heading away from Enychi's school, I noticed a big dude that looked just like that nigga Tone, on a Suzuki bike heading in the same direction I just left from.

Hold the fuck up! I made a U-turn, drove on a bit, and parked my car crossways from Enychi's school. Watching her face light up at the sight of Tone, as she kissed his lips the way she used to kiss mine, had me vexed. I couldn't believe this bitch was skipping out of classes that I was paying for, to creep around with that muthafucka. She threw on his spare helmet, hopped her ass on the back of that nigga's bike, and they took off like they was down with the Ruff Riders clique.

I kept my distance and followed them to a Brooklyn movie theater. I peeked down at my watch: It was eleven A.M. *Who fucks with a movie at that time of morning?* I thought.

Immediately after they purchased their tickets I entered the empty theater. I saw them go into theater number 9, "The Diary of a Mad Black Women."

I bought my ticket and fucked around with the video games for about fifteen minutes or so, playing a little Mortal Kombat just until the previews finished and the lights were out.

When I walked inside the theater it was dark, but it didn't take long for me to spot them, because they were the only two in there. Enychi wouldn't have noticed me or anyone else, because she was already too busy, on her knees.

Tone's head was leaned back and his eyes were closed. He looked like he was in fuckin' bliss, so it wasn't hard to figure out what was going on. Especially since I knew what it felt like to have my dick in her mouth, too. I got on some sneaky shit myself, dipping down low in the aisle until I found the best seat in the house directly behind them, two rows back.

I watched my chick bounce up and down on that nigga's dick like she was a professional, fuckin' bull rider. A voice in my head said *Damn, you wanted the truth. Well, here's some truth for ya ass.* My blood boiled and tears watered my eyes, but I let them rock.

Staring at the two of them only angered me more, as all the woulda, coulda, shouldas invaded my brain. I only had myself to blame.

Instead of telling that nigga to suck my dick, I welcomed him to my girl. I knew I didn't handle Tone like a real man was supposed to, so I can't even be mad at him for snatching her up.

It's real when they say that the same thing that makes you laugh can also make you cry, 'cause Enychi brought joy to my life. I loved the hell outta her. Right then, I was feeling fucked up, crying on the inside and out, while that nigga Tone was getting his laugh on. It was going down like that and it wasn't shit I could do about it. So I did what a smart nigga would've done, I got up and got the fuck up out of there.

"Fuck the both of them," I told myself, as I did about a hundred on the Belt Parkway. All type of thoughts were playing tug-of-war in my head. I wished I would've done things differently, but since I didn't, fuck it! I had to deal with it; why go to jail over some pussy I ain't fucking.

Once I got back to the crib, the anger, pain, and regret I was feeling started to get the best of me. I balled up my fist and punched the wall so hard that I broke the skin on my knuckles. "Fuck!" I yelled, fanning my stinging hand from side to side. I fell onto the couch and sparked up some strong-ass weed, hoping it would numb my pain. After a few drags from the blunt, I rested my head back on the pillow. Immediately feeling high and almost relaxed, I started thinking about the first time I met Enychi. It was the same day I came home from jail two years ago.

I remember waking up at the break of dawn, feeling excited because my freedom was just couple of hours away. I couldn't wait to get the hell up out that dingy-ass jail cell. All I kept thinking was, *Damn, I hope Mel be out there when I get out.* The loud sound that the prison outer gates made as they opened sounded just as good as listening to a hot-ass Biggie joint for the first time. I was hype as I strutted up outta there. With my head held high, looking up at the sky, I took a whiff of fresh September air and smiled. I swear I could hear the words of the late great Martin Luther King in my head: *Free at last, free at last, thank God Almighty—a nigga's free at last.*

Yes indeed, I was a free man once again. And just like I'd hoped, Mel was waiting outside the gates, posted up against his Z3 platinum-colored BMW.

"Damn, nigga, what took you so fucking long?" he said, smiling, like he was happy to see me coming up out of a bad situation.

"My nigga, my nigga!" I said as we gave each other a pound and swapped some brotherly love. "Damn, it feels good to be up outta that joint.

"Yo, dawg, that's you?" I asked, referring to the convertible hot ride that was sparkling like a diamond as the sun beamed down on it.

"Yeah, nigga, that's me. I've been trying to tell you. Yo, business is lovely, dawg!"

"Damn, I hear that."

"You hear that, nigga? You could be driving something like that," Mel said.

"Nah, man I ain't trying to get locked the fuck up again."

"Yeah, I hear you, dawg, but I'm doing shit on a whole 'nother level now, you feel me?

"But, 'ay, ain't no pressure. You stay shook and I'ma stay getting this paper, a'ight? You still my dawg." Mel sighed with disappointment, shaking his head as he headed over to the driver's side of his BMW and got in. "Come on, nigga, get in. Let's get the fuck up out of here." I sensed that Mel was a little tight about my decision not to hustle anymore, but I could tell he was trying his best to respect it.

Mel ripped through the highway doing 110 mph with the rooftop down, as his system pumped a Ron G mix tape. I reclined back in the seat while the fresh air cuffed my face, bopping my head to the sound of the music and enjoying the ride. I checked out the scenery for shit that might've changed since I was gone. Mel took me to get a bite to eat first. Next, we hit to the mall to tighten up my gear. Last, he pulled up in front of an apartment, handed me the keys, told me it was mines—and already furnished.

"Oh, and here's a couple of dollars for your pocket until you decide what you gon' do. You know, until you get on ya feet," he added.

I looked at the fist-sized, mixed knot of twenties, fifties, and hundreds, and thought, *A couple of dollars? Damn, this nigga must really be getting it.*

"Yo, Mel, you know you my dawg, right? Man, thanks for looking out," I told him because I felt so grateful for a friend like him.

"Nigga; you know I got you, at least until you stop tripping and get back on with me—but anyway, go take a hot shower, 'cause we both know that ain't something you did by yourself in a while," Mel teased.

"Oh, you got jokes, huh!" I laughed vigorously.

"Nah, nigga; but seriously, rest ya head for a minute, get right, do what you gotta do, and then come through the projects. You know where my moms stay at, right?"

"Come on, nigga, I ain't been gone that long," I answered sarcastically.

"A'ight, cool. Come through then, 'cause I'm putting together a little welcome home sumptin-sumptin in the back of the building, you know what I mean?"

"A'ight, that's what's up! I'ma be through."

"A'ight, my nigga, see you then. And, hey, I'm glad you home, man."

"No doubt, I'm glad to be home!" I added.

Later that night, when I crept on the scene, the night air was nice but a little breezy. Still, damn near the whole projects was hanging out to enjoy it.

The DJ was in the middle of an old-school set, as the party jumped to Eric B and Rakim's classic, "Paid in Full." I felt like a kid again, cheesing from ear to ear when I saw helium balloons, swaying from side to side through the air, that read "Welcome Home." On top of that, Mel's moms was getting busy on the grill, flipping steaks, hotdogs, chicken, and burgers. She had it smelling like she knew what she was doing, too, as I walked over to say hello to her.

Mel's mom, Ms. Aubrey, was an attractive forty-something-year-old woman, and could easily be mistaken for a much younger one, with her ghetto-fabulous attitude and style. She tried a little too hard to uphold her youthfulness, as she posed in front of the grill in some tight army fatigue–printed booty shorts that exposed the dark part of her ass cheeks, and cleavage oozing from her matching tank top. Her makeup was flawless, and Mel saw to it that her neck, ears, and wrists blinged flamboyantly with plenty of diamonds and gold.

"Welcome home, Wasuan." She greeted me with a tight hug. "You looking scrumptious! Did you see your mother yet? I was hoping she would come, but I think she's still a little upset with everything, you know?"

"Yeah, I know," I said quickly, not trying to get into a discussion about the woman who didn't write me one letter or come to see me while I was locked up. As far as I was concerned, I didn't have a mother. Yeah, I loved her, but she couldn't see past the flaws of my father, and I wasn't going to force her to.

Suddenly Mel walked up, threw his arm across my shoulders, and dragged me away.

"C'm'ere, nigga, I know you ain't tryna holla at my moms." He threw back his head and laughed. "Nah, just kidding; but what up with a game of c-lo for old time sake."

"What, kid? You don't wanna fuck with me and that dice shit. Nigga, you thought my roll game was bananas before, well it's off the meter now!"

"A'ight, nigga, we'll see," Mel challenged, as he laughed and signaled for a few of his boys to come over and play.

"Yeah, we gon' see, but don't start crying once I take your money, dawg, and them niggas, too." I chuckled and pulled out three brand new dice that I'd brought on my way over in hopes that a game would go down. It felt good to shoot dice on the streets again. Assuming that I was probably a little rusty, niggas were dropping fifty- and hundred-dollar bills into the pot.

"Y'all niggas running up and throwing around big bills and shit? Mel, I see you ain't schooled these dudes. Oh, what? Y'all niggas just got paper to blow like that, huh? That's what's up?

'Cause the kid is back, baby. Check my résumé, yo."

Once some of the fellas heard my mouth, they knew what time it was. A group of them started going back and forth at each other, selling wolf tickets. A few argued "The boy is nice" in my defense, while others slept on how good I really was.

"Nigga, you can't be that nice. Nice niggas don't talk that much," one of the dudes yelled out at me.

"A'ight, then I'm done talking. You got your money up, right?" I had butterflies in the pit of my stomach and it wasn't 'cause I was nervous. I wasn't just talking. I lived for the game, the shit talk, and the haters that doubted how nice I was.

"What up? Anybody else wanna to lose some money up in dis bitch?" I said sarcastically; but niggas ain't want it with me.

I was cheesing from ear to ear as I straightened my dough out, thinking, *That shit was too easy*. I made a quick six hundred for my pocket, and was ready to get my eat and drink on. As I walked over to the liquor table, I saw her and was stuck. "Damn, she's bad," I said out loud to myself. I couldn't help but do a double take as I walked over to Mel. "Yo, Mel, who's that?" I questioned, nudging my boy in the arm with my elbow.

"I don't know, but she's a friend of 'Nita's. Why? You like her?" Mel asked.

"Hell, yeah, I like her."

Mel shrugged his shoulder. "Yeah, she's definitely a ten." He was real casual about it, as he took a swig of his Corona.

Once that nigga Mel started getting money, pretty chicks ain't phase him no more, and he was mainly into the light-skin women; but, to me, shorty was more than a ten. As a matter of fact, I ain't never seen beauty like hers before, not even in a dream.

"Yo, you think you can get your sister to hook that up for me?" I asked him.

"Dawg, I know you need some pussy, fresh out of jail and all, but I don't think you heard me. She's friends with my sister, so you know what that means, yo?"

I had no clue what that meant and couldn't think of anything that would matter. My eyes followed the girl's every move.

"Yo," Mel waved his hand in front of my face, breaking my stare, "dawg, you know my sister is one bougie-ass bitch, so that means she gotta be one, too. Trust me, yo, don't even set yourself up for the rejection."

"Fuck that. I ain't scared of no rejection. I'll take my chances." I walked away from Mel and made my way towards her. To me, the closer I got the better she looked, I started getting nervous. As Denita engaged in girl talk with Miss Chocolate Delight, I prepared myself for the worst and prayed that she would give me some play. Clearing my throat, I thought about my plan. I'd walk up to Denita and hopefully ease my way into their conversation.

"What up, 'Nita?" I hit her with my thousand-watt smile. "How you been?"

"I'm good! Welcome home." Denita leaned in and gave me a hug.

After her hug I lingered around, hoping she'd introduced me to her homegirl. After about sixty seconds, Denita must've caught on, because she finally turned to me and said, "Oh, excuse my rudeness. Wasuan, this is my friend Enychi. Enychi, this is my brother's homeboy, Wasuan, the man of the hour." She said it with very little enthusiasm. I licked my lips like I was

---

LL, and then I hit her with my killer smile. "How you doing, Enychi?" I said as I extended my hand.

"I'm good, and yourself?" she answered back in the sweetest tone, as she gave me a delicate handshake. I could tell the way she seemed so indifferent that she had to be used to guys trying to hit on her all the time.

"Hey, girl, I'm going in front of the building. You coming, or what?" Denita asked as she twisted up her mouth.

"Yo, go ahead. She a'ight, 'Nita." I couldn't believe Denita. Here she was trying to cock block, knowing that a nigga was fresh out the joint. If anything, I felt she should have taken it upon herself and looked out for me.

My heart was crushed when Enychi said, "Well, it was nice meeting you," and then walked off following Denita.

Mel laughed as I walked back towards him empty-handed. "Nigga, I told you!" he said.

"Man, fuck you! If it wasn't for your hatin'-ass sister, I could've pulled that."

"Yeah, right!" Mel turned up his lips and sucked his teeth. "If you can pull that, I'll give you twenty-five hunnid right now."

"Twenty-five hundred? Right now?" I repeated.

"Yep, two thousand, five hunnid, nigga. If you can get shorty number right now!" For assurance he dug in his pocket and pulled out his knot of cash and began to peel off hundreds.

"Bet. I'll be right back to collect that." I walked off in search of Enychi. I weaved my way through the bobbing crowd of dancers and, when I didn't see her in the crowd, I rushed out to the front of the building.

"Yo, yo, yo! Hold up a minute," I yelled out to the cab driver, whose backseat Enychi was climbing into. I handed the driver a twenty-dollar bill and asked if he'd wait for just a few moments. The cabbie agreed, but Enychi wasn't too thrilled. "Excuse me! What are you doing?" she snapped.

Before I could explain my actions, a loud *boc, boc, boc,* came from the back, along with the sounds of people screaming, "They shooting!" "Run!" "Get down!" "Where's Man-Man? Grab TeeTee!" immediately followed by a stampede of feet.

I pushed Enychi in the car and hopped in next to her. "Drive!" I yelled at the cabbie as the partygoers began to scatter, dodging bullets. People ran in all directions, while a few jumped in vehicles and sped off. Enychi was scared to death. I could tell by her behavior that she wasn't used to the sound of gunfire.

"Oh, my god." Enychi placed her hand over her chest. She gasped for air as if she was trying to get herself together. Turning to face me, her expression of panic changed to anger. "What the hell are you doing?" she screamed out, sounding more annoyed than the first time she'd asked that question.

"I thought I was making sure you was safe." Her reaction had me puzzled.

"Okay, well, I'm safe now—and I probably would have been home by now, if you didn't stop the cab in the first place! So, umm, driver, at the next light can you please pull over and let this gentleman out?" Enychi's ungratefulness, along with her attitude, was off the hook to me.

"Nah, cabbie, I got you! Just take shorty to her destination. Yo, check this out, Enychi, is it?" I knew it was time to just let her know what I was feeling.

She rolled her eyes as she answered, "Yes?"

"I ain't mean no harm. All I wanted was a few moments of

your time, so you could hear me out. And then if you still ain't tryna hear what I'm saying, you don't have to see me again, a'ight?"

Enychi didn't verbally respond to me, but the way she folded her arms and twisted up her face, I could see she wasn't trying to hear nothing I had to say. But I was gonna give it a try anyway. She was so feisty, I wasn't sure what turned me on more, her beauty or her attitude.

Enychi didn't say anything, she just looked at me with those beautiful, chinky eyes of hers. I must admit I couldn't help but get a little tongue-tied. "Damn, girl," I said, "you got me feeling more nervous now than I did when they was shooting, but fuck it, I gotta get this off my chest."

Enychi started tapping her leg, then looking at her watch and out the window for the remainder of her ride. Again, I caught and ignored the message. "Look, it ain't hard to tell. I know cats come at you all the time with every weak-ass line in the book, but that ain't me, I ain't got a line. I'ma just keep it real with you. I think you're beautiful and I wanna to get to know you better. So, can I—please?"

Enychi sat quiet for a moment, and I might've thought she was giving what I said some thought. Instead, she was just trying to hold on to her response long enough for the cab to approach her stop. After a few seconds, she let out a hard sigh. "Listen, whatever your name is, don't take this personal, but I'm really not interested. Besides, I have a lot on my plate right now."

She shut me down and my heart dropped. Imagining that was what rejection felt like, I wasn't cool with the feeling at all; but, nevertheless, I was a persistent muthafucka, and my pride wasn't gonna let me accept that as her final answer, so I asked her "What, you got a man?"

And she answered coldheartedly, "No, I don't have a man. I just don't have time for you to get to know me, that's all."

"Wow, it's like that?" That night I gave up; I wasn't going to tussle with Enychi's diva-ass attitude anymore. "A'ight then. Fuck it!" I added with an attitude of my own, ready to just let her ass go.

"Right here is fine, driver!" Enychi said as she ignored my comment. The cabbie came to a screeching stop and pulled over, and she eagerly made her exit without a word, then slammed the car door and walked off.

"Good night to you, too," I mumbled under my breath. Then it dawned on me "Oh, shit, Mel!" I had left Mel at the party. "Yo, take me back to the projects," I instructed the driver.

Once the cab reached the buildings, there were about eight cop cars and two ambulances parked in the middle of the street. I handed another twenty to the driver. "Just give me five minutes, a'ight?" I said, as I hopped out the car.

Walking up to the barricade, I told a woman officer that my people lived in the building and I needed to make sure they were all right. It took some convincing, but finally the cop let me through. My main focus was making sure that Mel and his family was all right.

Mel wasn't only my nigga, but also my lifeline in the 'hood. Rushing past police, I made my way to the back of the building, where I saw the coroners pull the first stretcher out from the back. On it there was a dead person, already in a body bag. My stomach felt weak and my heart raced as I thought the worse.

Suddenly I heard the raspy voice of Mel cussin' someone out. "I said I was a'ight. I'm not going to no fuckin' hospital. Just wrap my shit up. I'll live." Mel was being pushed out in a wheel-chair by one of the EMS workers. Through all the onlookers he was able to find my face.

"Hey, nigga, you see they got me strapped down in this fuckin' wheelchair, like a nigga really hurt the fuck up," Mel said to me. I later found out that, during the chaos, Mel got cut on his leg pretty badly from a broken beer bottle.

"Damn, nigga, let them do their job," I said, relieved that my boy's injuries were minor and that he was okay.

"Nah, I don't want them to do their bullshit-ass job. I just want them to patch my shit up so I can handle my business."

I couldn't help but laugh. I hadn't been out a full twenty-four hours yet, and already I'd had a night filled with drama. "Yo, it's been a long night. What happened?"

"Ay, man, you know when you get a bunch of niggas to-gether they don't know how to act. All I know is, for the most part, I'm good, you good, my fam's good, so I'm a'ight. You good, right? You need a ride, nigga?"

"Nah, I'm good. I got a cab waiting. Let them patch you up, nigga, and you know where I'm at if you need me." I patted Mel on the shoulder and walked toward the waiting cab.

When I got to my apartment, I stretched across my queen-size bed and imagined Enychi lying right beside me. Thinking about her beauty, the sweet smell of her perfume, and her feisti-ness gave my dick an instant hard-on. I removed my third leg from my jeans and started to firmly stroke it, as my mind drifted off into a much more graphic fantasy. Masturbating to the thought of fucking Enychi felt incredible. I could almost feel the warmth of her dripping wet pussy, and even my mouth watered for a taste. The head of my dick swelled as that last stroke caused my cum to shoot out of me like a rocket. "Damn, you're the greatest," I sighed, as if Enychi had actual took part in my moment of ecstasy. No woman had ever caught my attention like that before, I realized, as I dozed off into a good, deep sleep.

At the sound of Enychi's keys rattling in the apartment door, I sat up on the couch with all types of scenarios of how to confront her running through my mind. My first reaction was to run up on her with a right hook and then stomp the shit out of her once she hit the floor. But that wasn't my style, my pops never put his hands on my moms, so I wasn't gonna do it to Enychi, no matter how much she deserved a beat down. So I chilled, and took the laid-back approach as she walked through the door with her backpack hanging off her shoulder.

"Hey," Enychi said in a dry-ass tone.

"What's up? How was class today?" I asked, curious to hear her answer.

Enychi nervously smoothed her hand over her hair and looked away. "It was all right. One of my teachers sprung a pop quiz on us, but I think I did okay."

"You think?"

"Nah, I'm pretty sure I did okay." Enychi dropped her books down on the coffee table.

Whatever happened to honesty being the best policy? I couldn't believe that this was the same chick I'd met two years ago. I really felt like kicking her ass for real, but I was gonna give her more rope to hang herself with first.

"Anyway, I'm tired," she said, yawning. "I'ma go take me a hot shower and then a nap." Enychi started walking towards the bathroom.

"Nah, hold up a minute. I wanted to holla at you. I was gonna last night, but you must've been tired then, too, since you ain't hear me come in or feel me snuggle up next to you."

"Hoo," Enychi exhaled loudly. "You can't wait until later, Wasuan?"

"Nah, I already waited until today. So I'ma say what I gotta say and then you can go do what you gotta do." Enychi was really playing me, talking about taking a shower—she should've washed that nigga off of her scandalous ass before she brought it up in here.

Enychi walked back into the living room with a slow drag in her step and leaned up against the wall across from where I was sitting. She had the nerve to stand with her arms folded and a bothered look on her face.

"Yeah, so like I was saying, I wanted to talk to you since last night, to see how we can try and fix this shit between us." As I spoke, Enychi rolled her eyes up in her head like she could give two shits about what I was saying. I took a deep breath to keep from spazzing out on her ass. Barely grabbing ahold of myself, I continued. "I wanted to get shit right with us, but I could see our shit's dead now, ain't that right, Nych?"

"I don't know, you tell me?"

"Come on, Nych, man, just tell me the truth. Be real with your shit. I mean, you can't even stand here and have a conversation with me without a fuckin' attitude, right? So let's stop with the games. Tell me what's up?"

"Tell you what's up with what?" Enychi started fidgeting with her fingers.

"You know what! You the one that's been walking around here wearing your ass up on your shoulders, like I did something to you. And all along, you fuckin' that nigga Tone. You was fuckin' him all this time, wasn't you?" My blood boiled as I stared at her.

"Here you go again with that Tone bullshit. I'm going to bed!"

I charged at Enychi as she was finishing her words. "You ain't going nowhere." I lost it and wrapped both my hands around her neck and slammed her against the wall.

"Get off of me, Wasuan!" she screamed, with a look of shock on her face.

"Tell me, just admit it! You a sneaky, lying-ass bitch! I already know! I followed you today!" My voice started to crack as I struggled to keep my emotions from showing.

"Let me go, Wasuan!"

I slammed her ass again. "Enychi, I'm not letting you go until you fuckin' tell me the truth. I seen you! I watched that nigga pick you up from school and how y'all got down in the movie theater. So just let me hear you say it, for my satisfaction!" I know I said hitting her wasn't my style, but fuck it! Her ass deserved it. Shit, she's lucky all I was doing was hemming her ass up by her neck.

"Okay, you wanna know the truth?" Enychi's eyes started to water. "I'll tell you truth. I'm fucking him every chance I get! You happy now, you sorry muthafucka? Now get off of me!" she yelled as she yanked at my hands.

I blanked out for about ten seconds, thinking, *should I take my hands from around her neck or listen to the voice in my head, say-*

ing 'kill the bitch' and rock-a-bye her ass to sleep? I already felt like a
sucker for letting Tone play me out, so taking my frustration out
on Enychi's ass might've made me feel a whole lot better. But
was it worth me going back to jail? Hell, no! So I came to my
senses and released her with a push. "You know what? Pack your
shit up and get the fuck out! Go be with that nigga, I'm done
with you."

"I will. Besides, I *been* done with your punk ass! At least he's
a real man," Enychi said with that slick-ass mouth of hers.

And damn, did that hurt. I tightened my fist up for that
comment, but instead of entertaining all that mouth she had, I
did us both a favor and freed myself from the crib—because I
was seconds away from seriously hurting her.

For a while I just drove around aimlessly, trying to sort out
some things in my head that were fuckin' with me. How did my
life come to this?

For years I looked for and held onto some ill feeling towards
my moms. I was mad as hell at her when she kicked me out at
eighteen; I hated her for not writing or coming to see me while I
was in lockup, and more than anything, I despised her for bailing
out on my pops. For me, that's when it all started. My moms
could ride a nigga too hard sometimes. It was like, she stayed mad
at my pops all the time for nothing. And as a kid, and sometimes
now, I never understood what her beef with him was about. I
mean, I looked at it as, so what if he gambled every now and
then? The bills got paid.

Pop was on his job when it came to taking care of home

and providing for us. He worked for the Metropolitan Transit Authority as a train engineer, and never once did he take a day off from his job. We lived in a middle-class neighborhood in St. Albans, Queens, in a four-bedroom house that Pops busted his ass to pay for. Meanwhile, my mom was a registered nurse, but all her paychecks went straight to her savings account.

I remember, every night I would sit by the door and wait for my pops to come home from a hard day's work. On the nights he showed up, he would come in with a big grin on his face as he held out his hand. "Gimme five," he'd say, and as soon as I slammed my small hand into the palm of his, Pops would hug me tight and say, "That's my boy"—every time. Then he'd walk up to my moms and kiss her face, kick off his shoes, wash his hands, and, as a family, we'd sit to the table, bless the meal, and enjoy eating together. After dinner, I'd follow Pops into the living room, squeeze my little body right beside him in his favorite brown-leather La-Z-Boy recliner, and we'd watch the six-o'clock news.

I appreciated those nights spent with my pops, because there were quite a few nights when he didn't make it home in time for dinner, the six o'clock news, or my bedtime. That's when I had to deal with my mom's attitude. She'd slam down pots as she put the food away and take her frustrations out on the next best thing—me. Especially if she caught me waiting by the door for my pops after she already put dinner up. She'd scream at me like she was nuts. "Boy, take your ass to bed! Your father's out somewhere gambling, so get away from that door. He ain't bringing his ass in here no time soon!" I would run to my room, get in bed, and force myself to sleep just to stay out her way, but in the middle of the night I'd wake up to her screamimg at my pops. Pops wasn't with all the yelling and screaming she did, so that caused him to stay out later and later, or come in drunk, just to tune her out.

Eventually, without warning, Pops told me that my moms packed his shit, waited up for him to come in from a late night of gambling, and told him he had to leave. He explained that it was for the best, because he was tired of her always complaining, and somehow separating didn't sound like such a bad idea. So, without hesitation, he left, and shortly after they divorced.

Since Pops had me on the weekends, I got exposed to a lot of his gambling. After actually seeing him shoot dice and admiring his style, it didn't take long for my interest to take flight. I wanted to learn how to roll just like Pops, and he was honored to teach me. While some fathers might've taught their sons how to play football or basketball, how to fix a car, or how to pick up chicks, my pops was different. His skills weren't on the court; he was too sharp to fix anybody's car, and the women were so turned on by his cool-ass style that they threw themselves at his feet, so that took very little effort on his part. His talent was gambling. Sure, it involved a bit of luck, but Pops knew that he had a great deal of skill to match, so he took me up under his wing and taught me how to master the game.

I remember one Saturday afternoon, when Pops took me to a spot that him and his buddies called "the number hole." That's where he spent most of his time at. The number hole was run as a members-only club. It had to be, to minimize the risk of getting busted for all the illegal gambling that went on inside. In my eyes, there was nothing special about the dingy, fire-hazardous, one-way-in, one-way-out hole in the wall, but my pops would always say you could walk up outta that hole in the wall with a nice piece of change, if you brought some luck witcha.

In the back of the spot there were two rooms, one was a small bathroom that reeked from the smell of strong piss, and the other was a room where all the other prohibited activities took place, such as blackjack, spades, dominos, and craps, along with plenty of drug and alcohol use as well. The number hole wasn't no place for an eight-year-old to be hanging out at, but since Pops had been broken in by *his* old man in a place just like it when he was a boy, he didn't see any harm in it.

He started me off by teaching me to observe and remember each player's strategy. I listened attentively as he instructed me to "hold the dice in your hand like this." Pops would let me roll a few of his shots, and from that day forward, it was on.

As though in a daze, I ended up parked outside of my mom's house, feeling like I had nowhere else to go.

E N Y C H I

As soon as Wasuan walked up outta here, I let go of that tough-girl act and burst into tears. *How did something that started off so good end up so bad?* We must've been crazy to think we could go back to the way things use to be.

In my mind, I'd seen this day coming, and I had been prepared to deny everything whenever he approached me about it, too. Only, Wasuan grabbing me by my throat like he did was unexpected. I didn't mean to blurt out what I said, but he was hurting me. I never meant for it to go down like it did, and not in a million years did I think Wasuan would just kick me out like that. I imagined he would be very upset, but then I'd blame him, agree to stop seeing Tone, and together we'd work it out. Silly me. Now what?

I grabbed three large garbage bags from the kitchen cabinet and started with the bedroom. Stuffing as much as I could into each bag, I didn't realize before now how many clothes I had. I knew I was gonna have to make another trip to get the rest of my things, but for now I was gonna take what I'd need the most.

On second thought, I was sure it would be best for the both of us if I just took all my stuff in one trip. So I decided to call Denita to see if she could borrow her mom's car to come and give me a hand.

"Hello," Denita answered immediately.

"Hey, 'Nita," I whined.

"What's wrong with you?" Denita asked sympathetically.

"Um, do you think you can borrow your mom's car and come give me a hand?"

"Ahh, what you need a hand with?"

"My stuff."

"Why, what happened?" she asked.

"Wasuan found out about me and Tone."

"Oh shit! How?"

" 'Nita, can you please just find out if you can get her car and come help?" I wasn't in the mood to feed her inquiring mind.

"Alright! I got my brother's hooptie. I'm on my way—okay?"

"Thanks."

Twenty minutes later, Denita was downstairs ringing the intercom. After I buzzed her in, I opened up the apartment door and waited for her to get off the elevator.

"Hey, girl, I hope they ain't gon' tow my brother's car," Denita said, walking off the elevator.

"Why? You parked on the ramp?"

"Yeah."

"Well, I got some stuff already packed. You can take those bags for me."

"Okay, cool. Now tell me, what happened?"

"Girl, I don't know. I came home and he just went off. He said he followed me today."

"Followed you? You was with Tone today, right?"

"Yes, 'Nita!" I snapped as my emotions took hold of me.

"Come on, Enychi, don't cry over his ass. Wasuan brought this on himself." Denita wrapped her arms around me and stroked my back.

"I know; but he was good to me. I didn't have to do him dirty like that."

"Fuck him!" she said, placing her hands on my shoulders. "Look at me, Enychi: What kind of man is gonna ask his girl to sleep with another dude if he loves her? He's a coward. So what, he was good to you? He was supposed to be! You cooked his meals, kept the place clean, and was fuckin' him. So, stop making excuses for his tired ass. You've given that nigga way too much credit. Wasuan got a problem, girl. If he'll gamble with his relationship, then he'll gamble with anything. And what's gon' happen the next time he get in another nigga's debt—what you gon' do, sleep with them too? Enychi, Wasuan did it to himself, so now he gotta suffer the consequences for his actions."

"You're right, Denita. I just didn't want him to think I was sleeping with Tone all this time."

"Enychi, why do you care what he thinks?" Denita sighed and shook her head like she was getting frustrated. "Anyway, let's get this stuff downstairs, before they tow my brother's car. You coming to my house, or what? 'Cause you know my moms won't mind."

"Uh-uh. You know Wasuan probably already told your brother what happened."

"And? So what! My brother don't live with us. Besides, I'm sure he'll agree that Wasuan played himself with that shit, too."

"But still, Wasuan and Mel are boys, so I wouldn't feel comfortable running into him right now. I'll just stay with Tone. I mean, he *is* part of the reason I don't have a place to stay, right?"

"You're right. Suit yourself; but if that nigga wanna act up, too, you're welcome to stay with us."

"Thanks, girl!" After Denita pulled off, I rushed back upstairs to finish packing the last of my belongings. As I was just about done, I thought it would be wise to stop what I was doing, locate my cell phone, and call Tone to let him know that I needed to crash with him for a little while.

"What up, ma?" he answered.

"Hey, baby—umm. I need to talk!"

"About what? You a'ight?"

"Not exactly, I need a place to stay for a minute."

"Why, what's going on?"

"Wasuan told me to leave. He knows about us."

"Yo, fuck that dude. I got you, ma. Where you at now?"

"I'm still at the apartment."

"Is he there with you?"

"Nah, he left."

"A'ight, yo, just go to that spot we went to yesterday near the airport, and wait for me. I'ma head over there in about fifteen minutes. A'ight, you cool with that?"

"Yeah, I'm cool with that!"

"A'ight, and don't sweat that shit. We'll work it out. Hurry up outta that nigga's crib and I'ma see you in a little bit."

"All right." I slammed the hood of my cell phone and I made my way to the door with the rest of my things. *Well, this is it.* Shaking my head, I took one last look around the apartment and left the keys, the memories, and Wasuan behind.

WASUAN

I sat outside of my mom's crib for about thirty minutes, wondering what her reaction was gonna be when she opened the door and saw me standing on her front step. Would she reject me? I couldn't even call it; but it was time to find out. Besides, it was now or never for me, and I had to get this shit off my chest right now. I got out the car, walked up to her doorstep, and rang the bell. I waited impatiently for a couple of seconds and then pressed down on the bell again. When I finally saw someone peek through the mini blinds, shortly after, I heard the door unlocking. My mother opened the door with a surprised look on her face. To me she still looked the same, only instead of strands of gray hairs she had a headful. Her eyes started to water as she stood in the doorway and looked me over without saying a word.

Out of nowhere, I broke down right where I stood.

"I'm sorry, Ma," I blurted out, damn near in tears myself. "Ahh—man, Ma, I'm sorry for everything I've done wrong." I was hurting inside, and I needed something I ain't had in a long time. I needed that love and special attention that only a mother can give. I needed to hear her tell me that everything was gonna be alright. My moms looked at me as if she could feel my pain, and without hesistation she took me in her arms and held onto me tight.

"Shh. Its okay, son. Whatever it is, it's gonna be okay," she whispered softly in my ear as she caressed my shoulders.

I held onto her like my life depended on it, and all the warm feelings I felt for her when I was a kid, before all the drama, came back.

"Come inside, son." She released me and stepped to the side so I could walk in. "Are you hungry?" she asked.

"Nah, I'm good." I said as I walked through the foyer and into the dining room, noticing that most of the house still looked the same. "Ma, I'm not trying to keep you. I just needed to come over here so I could talk to you, get some things off my chest, that's all. I finally understand now."

My mom exhaled like, finally, her burden had been lifted, "I'm glad you do, son, I'm glad you do," she cried. "You're my only son, the only child I have in this world, and even though our relationship hasn't been on the right track for some time now, that doesn't mean I don't love you or I don't go to bed every night wondering, hoping, and praying that you're alright out there. I always cared and always will. I love you, Wasuan, and nothing will change that."

"Ma, I just don't know what's going on with me. So much bad shit, oh, my bad," I said as I apologized for the slipup and continued, "I mean, so much stuff is going on in my life right now, Ma. I don't know what to do! I'm trying hard to do the right thing out there in them streets because I don't wanna go back to jail. But it's like the devil is riding me hard. And I'm not sure I could fight him off me anymore.

"Outside of that, I love you, Ma, and I apologize for blaming you for all the things I had no business blaming you for. Up until today, I was blaming you for the way Pops's life turned out. I felt like you was the one responsible for his death. I thought you hated him, and that's why you ran him away. I never understood why you'd get so mad at me for emulating his style and wanting to be just like him. But I do now, 'cause, I *am* like him, Ma, and I'm sorry."

"Wasuan, I loved your father with all my heart; but I hated the fact that he put that damn gambling before me. Now, don't get me wrong, as far as taking care of the household he was a good provider; but when it came down to taking care of my personal needs, he wasn't never around. I started to feel like he loved tossing them dice around more then he loved me, his own wife. I just didn't understand how he could love something so much, and it couldn't love him back. So I said that's it—no more! I wasn't gonna live my life like that anymore. He let his addiction tear us apart, and later on it took his life.

"Then, when you got older, I'd come home and find you out on the street corner, or in front of my house, with those dice in your hand. I saw the same love in your eyes for gambling that your father had, every time I caught you playing. I'd run up on you and try hard to pry those dice out your hands, and you'd get so angry and hostile.

"It was Pop all over again, and I wasn't gon' sit back and watch you go down the same road he did with those same bad habits. But you just became so unruly and disrespectful towards me, and I wasn't tolerating that kind of behavior from anybody, let alone somebody I gave birth to. Wasuan, I had to put you out of here. It was either that or, honey, I was gon' hurt you," she said, as she looked at me like she was just that crazy to have done it.

"I know I was wilding out, but I just wanted to hold onto that part of Pops. I mean, he passed his gift down to me, and I knew if I was good at it like he was, he'd be proud of me."

"Wasuan, sometimes a person's gift can also be his curse, you know."

"I'm starting to see that now."

"Well, baby, that's a start. Wasuan, I just want you to make me proud, and that's not by running around in these streets dealing drugs, getting involved in them street gangs, or getting caught up in that gambling. That's why, when you went to jail, I had to turn my back on you, because I wasn't happy with how you was living your life, so I damn sure wasn't gonna act like it by giving you my support, not in there I wasn't."

I disagreed with that part, 'cause a letter from her every once in a while would've been nice, but if that's how she felt, that's how she felt. "I can't argue with that," I said quickly moving on. "Ma, I just wish I could take back so much, man, but I can't."

"Son, you can't dwell on your past mistakes. What's done is done. As long as you learn from your mistakes, you'll be all right. Now, come on over here and give your momma another hug."

I stood up and my moms wrapped her arms around me again. "I love you, son," she whispered softly.

"I love y—"

My words were interrupted by the sound of keys at the front door.

"Son, here comes someone that I really want you to meet. He's very special to me. In here, honey!" my moms called out, as her face lit up.

My pops's been dead for fifteen years, but still, I wasn't feeling another nigga being up in his crib or entertaining my moms. I couldn't even front like I was okay with it. Instantly, I screwed up my face as this tall, dark-skinned cat in about his early fifties walked into my mom's kitchen.

"Richard." She blushed as scrams kissed her on her lips. "Finally, I get to introduce you to my son, Wasuan," she said grinning from ear to ear.

I could tell from the look on her face that the two of us meeting meant a lot to my moms, but as what's-his-face extended his hand, I grilled him with a look that should've been deadly.

"Ma, no disrepect, but I ain't ready for this. I gotta go now, anyway!" I brushed past dude and made my way outta there, quick, fast, and in a hurry.

ENYCHI

"Twenty-five dollars. Excuse me, miss? Miss? That'll be twenty-five dollars," the Middle Eastern man said to me from behind the bulletproof glass partition.

"Oh, I'm sorry," I said, snapping out of my trance as I slipped the money under the slot. He placed the small bottle of Grey Goose in the turnstile and spun it around. I grabbed it and rushed from the store. I walked out just in time to see one of New York's finest traffic cops waddling towards my car, which just happened to be double-parked. I jumped in and sped off, thinking *A ticket is the last fucking thing I need right now.*

"Shit!" I screamed, as I made my way onto the Van Wyck Expressway and spotted all that damn rush-hour traffic. I hated being stuck in traffic. Sitting there made me so mad, and since I had nothing but time on my hands, I started to think about some things. Like why Tone suggested we meet at a hotel in the first place, when I told him I was gonna need to stay with him for awhile. As a matter of fact, I've never even been to his place. Shit, I was so caught up in my own creeping, that meeting up at a hotel seemed normal. But never once did I think about whether or not he was cheating, too. *Damn, what if he does have a girlfriend?* Well, I was about to find out.

Thankfully, as I got off the parkway, the hotel was only a few blocks away, because the way I was zoning out, I didn't need to drive any further. *Where is this nigga?* I thought when I pulled into the Wyndham's parking lot. It was cold as hell out that night, so Tone probably didn't have his bike; but I didn't see his Benz, either, as I drove through the lot. Actually, I was glad that he hadn't shown up yet. I needed a moment or two just to re-group. After backing into a space right in front of the hotel, I cracked open the bottle of Goose. I was never a hard-core drinker, but that night I needed a strong drink in the worst way. I took a hard swig from the liquor bottle, and boy did I regret it. My eyes got all watery and I couldn't stop coughing. I swear to God, I thought the vodka was going to burn a hole in my chest.

When I finally stopped gagging, the liquor sent a calming feeling throughout my body. I reclined my seat and rested my head against the headrest. Now my focus was coming back. So much shit was clogging my head the last couple of hours, I couldn't even sort out my thoughts. This thing with me and Tone was no longer some little creeping game. This shit was real! My relationship with Wasuan was now a complete wrap. Wa had thrown me out of *our* house like a used condom, the fucking nerve of him. Not to mention he put his hands on me . . . I mean, I know seeing me with Tone must've crushed him. But now that I think about it, so the fuck what! Like 'Nita said, he brought it all on his self, with his compulsive gambling ass. How the fuck he gon' use my pussy to pay a debt and not expect any repercussions?

It finally began to dawn on me, I ain't need no broke-down, coward-ass nigga for no man. He can choke me out, but couldn't stand up to a nigga in the street. "Fuck you, Wasuan! Fuck you!" I yelled over and over again while banging my hand against the steering wheel. Feeling the tears gathering in the corners of my eyes, I picked up the bottle and took another swig. This time it didn't burn so bad.

"I look a mess," I mumbled, catching a glimpse of myself in the rearview mirror. My hair was all frizzy, my eyes were red and puffy from crying, and I had marks and scratches all over my neck. In an attempt to make myself look halfway presentable, I grabbed the brush from my purse. I brushed my hair back and pinned it into a neat bun.

I've become my mother, only worse, I thought, staring at my reflection in the mirror. What made it so bad is that I'd turned into the *stupid* version of her! At least she had the good sense to make sure her home and cars were paid for. Although she was no more than a two-bit church whore, my mother maintained a nice living from all the cash men had given her.

"Look at you," I said, still staring at myself in the mirror. "You're homeless and ain't got two cents to rub together. Yeah, you got this fly whip, but, hell, you can't even afford the payments. So what you gon' do now, huh? Trust and believe, I will not allow you to make the same mistake twice. If you're going to depend on another man, you better walk away with some shit to fall back on."

My phone rang, breaking up my lone conversation. "Yeah," I answered.

"Yo, ma, where you at?" Tone asked on the other end of the line.

"Sittin' at the hotel, waiting on you."

"I'm here in the lounge, having a drink."

"Oh, well, I don't see your car or your bike," I told him as I scanned the parking lot again.

"That's cause I'm in something different right now. Come in. I'm on my way to the lobby."

Tone signaled for me to come inside, once he walked into the lobby. I got out the car, and waved for him to come to me.

"What's wrong, ma?" Tone said, standing in the hotel's door.

"Nothing. It's just that all my stuff's in this car."

"Yeah, I see that, but we could bring all that up later."

"No, I don't wanna just leave my things piled in the car like this," I told him. Me being slightly demanding, I could tell Tone was a little aggravated—especially by the way I sighed before responding. "A'ight, ma. Let me go find one of those dudes that work here and see if he can unload your stuff and bring it to the room."

"Tone," I called out to him, stuck. I looked at him with uncertainty as he turned to me and answered.

"What?"

"Nothing. Never mind," I said, realizing that right now might not have been the best time to start asking questions. I began to unpack my things from my car and place them in the hotel's lobby.

"Yo, my man." Tone summoned the hotel bellman for help, and he came walking towards us, pushing one of those carts to load my stuff on.

As soon as we walked into the hotel room, I couldn't hold it in any longer. My desire to know whether or not Tone was already shacking up with someone was too strong to ignore. I wanted to know exactly what I was getting myself into.

"Tone, why didn't we meet up at your place? I know you don't expect me to live here, in a hotel room. And, if I was okay with staying here—which I'm not—I don't even have a job or any money to pay for this room."

"Ma, didn't I tell you, I got you? Just be easy. I'ma help you get a spot, a'ight? Chill."

Okay, maybe he didn't hear my first question. Let's try this again. "But in the meantime, why can't I stay with you?"

"Enychi, ma, come on. You up in here worrying about the wrong shit, yo." Tone removed his black, fitted Atlanta Braves baseball hat from his freshly done braids, and sat it on the nightstand next to the bed. "Can we just lay down with each other and relax?" he said, still ignoring the question.

"Tone, you live with somebody, don't you?" I pressed. "Be honest with me, please." At this point, him avoiding my question made his answer quite obvious.

Tone let out another one of those hard sighs, sat on the edge of the bed and buried his face in the palms of his hands. Seconds later he said, "It's not what you think, Enychi."

I cut my eyes at him and placed my hands on my hips. "Well, what is it then?" I said, thinking, *Here we go with his bullshit now.*

Staring down at the green-and-burgundy carpet, he massaged the top of his head. "Let me see, how I can break it down. Um." After moments of beating around the bush, Tone finally came clean. "I'm married, yo."

"What! I know you didn't just sit here and say you were married?" *Married.* I thought I was gonna pass out. I was almost prepared to hear him say he had a girl and, yes, they lived together. But marriage? That was the straw that broke the camel's back.

"Tone, how the fuck did you manage to leave such a big detail like that out? Married! How could you do this to me?" I yelled.

"Yo, it ain't even like that between me and and ol' girl no more. We got married while I was locked up, and she held me down for that ten years I did. But I ain't got the same kind of love for her I use to have. I feel obligated to stay with her, because all the other bitches I was fuckin' with was out before my arraignment; she stuck around, ready to ride it out with me. She know shit ain't the same no more. I can't sit here and say she's happy about it, but she lives comfortable. So we straight."

"I hear what you saying and all, but you still should've told me, Tone. I can't do this." All of a sudden there was a light tap at the door and Tone got up to open it. It was the bellman with my bags, a reminder that I had nowhere else to go.

Tone helped the man bring my belongings into the room and gave him a generous tip.

"Thank you, my friend," he said, smiling gratefully as he let himself out.

Tone looked at me. "So, what you was saying?" Picking up our discussion from were I left off he continued, "Oh, yeah, you can't do this, huh? Why, not? You already been doing it."

"I know, but I didn't know you had a wife."

"A'ight, well, I knew you had a man, so what's the difference? Besides, me having a wife don't change how I feel about you, so don't let it change what you feel for me."

"You probably got kids and shit, don't you?"

"Two little girls," he answered so low I could barely hear him.

"Two!" I repeated. "Ahh, damn! How did I get myself caught

up in this mess?" I flopped to the bed and buried my face in the pillow.

"Yo, ma, don't act like that!" Tone started to run his hand through my hair.

I lifted my face from the pillow. "Don't act like what? Like you don't have a wife and two kids at home waiting for you? Please, Tone." I sat up, "I should've just stayed with Wasuan."

The look on Tone's face turned ugly. "What the fuck you mean, you 'should've stayed with Wasuan?' Go back to that pussy-ass muthafucka then. I don't give a fuck!"

I sat there and fumed for a minute before pulling myself together. I was in no position to get on his bad side right now.

"I'm sorry. I didn't mean to say that," I said.

"Yeah, whatever! Don't ever throw that nigga up in my face again, you hear me? Shit, the way his punk-ass played you out, you shouldn't even fix your mouth to say no sucker shit like that."

If Wasuan played me out, then Tone was the fuckin' maestro overall, because he gamed both of us. So I know he ain't trying to act like the injured party. It didn't even matter, though. It wasn't about me and Wasuan anymore. This was about me, and right now I didn't have a pot to piss in or a window to throw it out of. I needed Tone, and that meant accepting his wife and all. I had made my bed, and now I had to lie in it. Only, this time I wouldn't be stupid about it and get caught napping without my *security*.

I got up off the bed and stood in between his legs. "Baby, honestly, I just said that to make you mad, that's all. I didn't mean it, I swear," I said smiling down at him.

"Yeah, well, you gon' make me mad, a'ight," he said with a *you got me with that one* smirk on his face, as he palmed my upper thighs with his hands and started to nudge my shirt up with his teeth.

I held my shirt up while Tone slid his tongue across the lower part of my belly.

"Ooh," I moaned. "You want me, don't you big daddy?" I could tell he liked for me to talk like that, because his dick caught an instant hard-on.

"Uh-huh. Take that shit off," he demanded, this time tugging at my jeans with his teeth as he started unbuckling his belt.

While I was still undressing, Tone grabbed me by my waist, tossed me onto the bed, and ripped my Vicki Secret undies off of me. I got mad for a hot minute 'cause those were a pair of my favorite, but as he put his face in the middle of my best-kept secret, all anger faded.

After we made love, Tone held me tight in his arms. As I laid on his chest I felt like it was the safest place on earth. But, slowly, reality set in again. After two years, it was really over between me and Wasuan, and I had given myself completely to Tone. The greatest love of my life was over now and there was no turning back. My emotions were all over the place. I was sad, scared, and confused, and I started to cry.

"Enychi, ma, what's wrong?" Tone asked when my tears hit his chest.

"Nothing. Just thinking, that's all."

"What you thinking about?"

I didn't answer for a long time. "You probably won't believe me, but Wasuan was my first," I finally said.

"First what? Cornball-ass nigga you fucked with?" Tone chuckled.

"Tone, I'm serious. Besides you, he's the only man I ever slept with."

"Ahh, come on, don't tell me that."

"But it's true."

"Yo, you really making me dislike dude. That nigga was the first nigga to hit it?"

"Yeah. I really thought he was the one for me."

"Nah, man, he ain't. That nigga's straight pussy. Yo, I should've shot him in his balls. On the real, I never liked that cat, and when I pulled out on his punk ass, I really thought he had some heart to go with all that mouth of his."

I thought back to the first night we went out, because he said he didn't threaten Wasuan's life. I stayed quiet about it. I had never believed Tone to begin with. I could tell by his attitude that he's the type to pull first and ask questions later.

"Anyway, fuck that nigga for real. Don't even bring his name up around me no more, a'ight?" Tone said, as he took me out of my comfort zone and got up and started picking up his clothes. "Listen, I gotta go. I still got some things I need to go and take care of before I call it a night."

I remained silent and just watched him while he dressed.

"Here's a few dollars in case you get hungry, a'ight? I'll be back in a few hours, okay?"

"All right, thanks." I was a little hesitant with my next question, because I didn't want to come off as a nag or even the needy type, but my curiosity about how his relationship with his wife really was forced me to ask. "Are you gonna spend all night with me when you come back?"

"Yo, didn't I tell you, I got you?"

"Uh-huh."

"A'ight then. You gotta trust me, ma." Tone kissed me on my lips and said, "When I come back, I'm all yours, all night. So keep it warm for daddy, a'ight?"

"Okay." I trusted he would come back tonight, but who knew about tomorrow or the next night? I could tell already that his whole married situation wasn't going to be easy.

Once Tone walked out the door, I glanced over at the night table where he left five crisp twenty-dollar bills.

Good ol' Earlene Carter, I thought laying back down in the bed. Even though I swore never to be anything like my mother, maybe it was my destiny to follow in her footsteps.

W A S U A N

As soon as I got back to my place and opened the door, I spotted Enychi's keys lying on the table. *What a fucking day!* I thought. First the you-me-and-he bullshit with Enychi, and now I gotta fucking deal with my moms having another man in her life, too. Man, if it ain't one thing it's another. And to top it off, I had a splitting-ass headache. But what fucked me up the most was walking into the bedroom and seeing the dresser drawers pulled out, closet doors wide open, and all Enychi's shit gone. She was really gone. Reality kicked me hard in the ass. I haven't felt pain like this since my pops died.

I laid down on the bed and tried to rest my aching head and forget everything, but Enychi's scent was on the pillows and the sheets and that only made my thoughts of her more profound. Like the first time I brought her to my crib.

Mel had decided at the last minute to put together a bash to welcome in the New Year. He said a new year always meant bigger and better things for him, so he wanted to bring it in with a bang.

And since Mel was flashy and loved a good party, he did it up big. On such short notice, he reserved a ballroom and a two-bedroom suite at the LaGuardia Marriott hotel in Queens. Mel made it happen and handled all the necessary details himself—from getting a DJ to sending the invitations out, which requested all-black attire—including shoes—with no exceptions.

The day before the party, Mel came and got me from my crib so we could hit the city to do some last-minute shopping for something to wear for his New Year's extravaganza that following night.

I hopped in the passenger side of Mel's Land Rover. "What up, nigga?" We tapped fist.

"Ain't shit. Just hoping we don't run into a whole lot of traffic, that's all."

"Yeah, I hope not, too. Man, a nigga starting to get excited about tomorrow night, though," I said.

"Yo, I'm telling you, the shit is gonna be on and poppin'. Man, I got so many muthafuckas coming, it's crazy. Yo, remember them bad-ass twin bitches Shakai and Shakima, that went to junior high with us—they coming, too." Mel sounded pretty excited his self.

"Word, Shakima is the one I wanted to holla at, right?" I asked while shuffling through Mel's CDs for some Jay-Z. Bouncing to his "Somehow, Some Way," we dipped in and out of traffic on the Van Wyck Expressway.

"Yo, I don't know who's who. Them bitches look too much alike; but I do know we got a big-ass hotel suite on the top floor of that bitch so we can get twisted, hit some skins, and be, like, 'next!' all night if we want, nigga!" Mel held out his hand for a pound.

"That's what's up," I agreed as our hands collided and we laughed. "Yo, I got a li'l dimepiece that I met the other day coming through."

"Word, from where?" Mel questioned.

"She said she from Baisley."

"Baisley Projects? Yo', if you hit that nigga, make sure you strap your joint up with two rubbers, word. What's her name?"

"Latavia. Why? You know her?" I asked.

"Nah, if that's her name, I don't think so. Just be careful fucking around with them bitches, 'cause they known for setting a nigga up."

"A'ight, but she seem like she cool."

"Nigga, they always do, until you wake the fuck up, butt-ass naked, handcuffed to the motel bed, and she gone, along with all your shit. But, nah, don't let me discourage you. The more hoes, the merrier. It's good to see you got over that bitch my sister be with."

"Enychi. Yeah, well, you know how that go. If you can't love the one you want, love the one you can get. Besides, she is too full of herself for me."

"I told you she was player, player." Mel threw back his head and laughed.

"Nah, nigga, you the player."

"Hell, yeah. And you should be too, instead of trying to fall in love and wife one these hoes. Man, I give a bitch a hundred and twenty seconds of affection, and if her shit is good, I might take her ass out to eat, or maybe slide her a couple of dollars, but that's it." Mel laughed again.

"A hundred and twenty seconds, that's it?" I asked.

"Yep, two minutes is all I'm givin' up."

"And that works for you?" I started laughing.

"All the time! I'm trying to tell you, if you spoon-feed these bitches a little at a time, they'll keep coming back for more." Mel extended his hand for some dap.

"I hear that," I said, slapping him five. My sights were still set on finding a good woman and sticking with her ass, but my nigga Mel was a funny dude.

The night of the party, I checked myself out in the full-length mirror on the front of my closet door, and a nigga was looking sharp. I had on some black Ralph Lauren tailored slacks, a black Ralph Lauren button-up, and a pair of black Cole Haan slip-on dress shoes. People always tell me I resembled A. I., but on the court, I couldn't ball for shit. If I could ball like him I'd be straight. Still, I felt like a celebrity that night, I was looking real Dapper Don. I admired myself for a few moments and was feeling the way I looked in dress clothes, because I was a straight baggy jeans, big shirts, and timberlands kind of dude, everyday. I put on a few squirts of Jean Paul Gaultier, and the ladies love it. Then I grabbed my black mink jacket and headed out the door.

On my way to the hotel I got aggravated, stuck on that congested-ass Van Wyck Expressway. Only thing that kept me sane was Hot 97 counting down the hits from 2002. I bopped my head as I listened to Puffy whining "he need a girl," then Usher telling a bitch "you ain't gotta call," while Nas rapped, "All I need is one mic."

Finally, at a quarter to ten, I pulled into the hotel parking lot. It wasn't hard to tell that many invited guests must have already arrived, because the lot was jammed. Entering the hotel for the first time, I looked around. *A'ight, Mel did a'ight*, I thought to myself, pleased with everything from the hotel's décor to the shine on the marble floors, and the exotic plants that stood tall in every corner of the lobby. I jetted toward the elevator doors as I saw them opening. Inside the elevator I heard the thumping bass coming from the ballroom on the lower level of the hotel's lobby. That shit had me ready to get my party on right then and there, but Mel wanted to chill in the suite until eleven and then make our grand entrance. When I got to the door, I did our recognizable one-two-three knock.

Mel ushered me into the two-bedroom suite. "What up, nigga?" he yelled with a half-empty pint-size bottle of Hennessy in his hand.

There was so much weed smoke in the air I had a hard time seeing what the room looked like when I walked in. "Yo, this shit is nice." I smiled, greeting the small group of fellas with a pound.

"Aye, yo, what up, homie?" Durty and Speedy said, lounging on the plush, multi-colored sofa, and, while chilling next to each other in the matching chairs, Jay nodded his hello and Chico was too caught up in the nice-size blunt he was puffing on to speak at all.

"Yeah, this spot is a'ight, man." Mel handed me a drink.

"Thanks, man. I see ya'll niggas already started the party." I sat down on the end of the cherry wood–colored coffee table, since it was the only available place left to sit in the living room area.

We killed time by cracking jokes on one another, getting high, taking nice-size shots of the yak to the head, and enjoying the outside view from the top-floor window.

Once the final hour arrived, we was ready to take our party to the bottom floor. As we approached the ballroom entrance, the famous DJ SML, from the Bronx, was undoubtedly putting it down on the wheels of steel, as he shouted Mel out for throwing such a banging-ass party.

Mel smiled hard when he entered the ballroom and saw a ratio of five women to one man. "Yo, let's get some drinks, nigga," he said, nudging me in the arm.

We strutted over to the bar and—I should of known—Mel's mom, Aubrey, was tending it. Even though the drinks were free, Ms. Aubrey fixed them to make sure niggas ain't fill up their cups with too much liquor at one time.

"There go my money-maker!" she called out to Mel. "Hey, son, don't worry, Mama holding it down. What's up? Um, y'all fly and shit tonight. So what y'all wanna sip on?" Aubrey said, flashing her gold-tooth smile.

"Thanks, Ms. Aubrey. You look pretty good yourself," I said, hitting her with a little flattery of my own.

"Honey, I look better than pretty good. How 'bout damn good? Oh, and Melone, I already told your sister, so I'm telling you now: I ain't nobody's momma tonight—okay, sweetie? It's a new year, and I'm tryna take one of these niggas home with me tonight."

"Ma, don't play yourself—and don't call me by that name. Give me and Wasuan a bottle of Moët, and push your tatas back down in that shirt, please," Mel demanded, with a hint of irritation to go with the embarrassment flushing his face.

"Wasuan, you see how your boy talks to me—like I'm one of his damn women!" Aubrey said, grabbing two bottles of champagne from the ice chest and passing them to me, and not Mel.

"Uh-uh. Don't just walk off. Give Mama a tip." She pointed to the glass jar set up on the bar, already filled with singles.

"What? A'ight. Here's a tip. You ain't my moms tonight, remember," Mel said snidely as he and I walked off, laughing.

We posed like celebrities for a moment, next to the DJ's setup; holding our bottles while scoping out the scenery, and then we popped the corks on the champagne and gulped right from the bottle.

"I'm sure glad I asked everyone to dress in black. Ooh, these some bad bitches in here." I knew Mel was pleased with his decision to make the event a black-tie affair, because, to him, a women in black was sexy, and as he looked around the room, I knew he saw some sexy chick, because I sure did.

"Yo, Mel, what time is it?" I asked, as he stared off into a crowd of women dancing amongst each other on the dance floor. "Yo, nigga, I ain't got my watch on. What time is it?" I asked his ass again, and he still ain't answer. One of them girls really had Mel's attention, 'cause the nigga look like he was drooling at the mouth.

"Damn, where she come from?" Mel finally broke his gaze and nudged me. "Yo, Wa, look at that light-skinned chick over there, standing by the door. Now that's a bad bitch right there," Mel said, slightly shrugging his head in the girl's direction.

"Oh, that's *me* right there, dawg! Remember the girl I was telling you about?" I smiled. "That's her." And indeed she was, standing over there with her small waist and thick, shapely legs in them high-ass high-heels she was wearing. I was just as pleased with her appearance as Mel was.

"Yo, word? The one from Baisley?" Mel inquired.

"Yep, that's Latavia."

"Wow, I thought I done fucked all the pretty yellow bitches in Queens. How the fuck did I miss her? She from B.P. for real?"

"That's what she told me," I said.

"Well, damn, nigga, don't keep her pretty ass waiting." Mel spoke in an envious but proud tone as we tapped bottles and I headed over to shorty.

Latavia was making her way over to the bar as I approached her, creeping up on her from behind. "Umm, you smell good!" I whispered in her ear.

Latavia quickly turned her head to see who I was. I had really caught her off guard. "Ooh, don't be running up on me like that. What if I woulda turned around swinging?" Latavia's smile was like sunshine, as she turned herself completely around to face me.

"I don't know. You mighta knocked me out, but since you didn't, where's my hug at?" She had a flirtatious look on her face as she stood on her tippy-toes and wrapped her arms around me. I had to bend my knees to embrace Latavia, 'cause I was six feet two—so I damn near buried her five-foot, two-inch frame in my chest. That's when I noticed Denita and Enychi standing right next to me, and for some reason I got nervous as hell. My heart felt like it had just dropped into the bottom of my stomach, as Enychi's and my eyes met.

I immediately removed my arms from around Latavia and suddenly felt like a nigga that just got busted for cheating. Of course, I knew that wasn't the case, but a nigga still couldn't shake off that uneasy feeling. I was loving Enychi's natural beauty and her conservative look, as she stood tall in a black, lacy blouse, some dark slacks, and a chic pair of round-toe pumps. I tried my best not to look at her, but at the same time, I caught her watching me when I did. I decided to have some fun with it, and flaunt Latavia in her face, just for the hell of it.

"What up, 'Nita?" I said, using Denita as my decoy, like always.

"Hey, Happy New Year!" Denita said to me, friendlier than usual because of the alcohol.

"The ball ain't drop yet, but what you sipping on?" I asked her.

"Alizé, you want some?"

"Nah I got what I need right here." I bit down on my lip, locked eyes with Latavia, and said, "But, yo, don't drink too much, okay, li'l sis?" Playfully winking at Denita, I grabbed shorty's hand and walked off without acknowledging Enychi's presence.

Just then the DJ lowered the music. "Aye, yo, it's about that time . . . so get them glasses filled to the rim and let's toast to 2003!" he said over the mic.

Everybody started to gather near them, as Ms Aubrey and Denita filled the empty champagne glasses lined up across the bar.

"All right, all right. Y'all got them glasses ready? Come on y'all—ten minutes left to the New Year. Let's get it popping," DJ SML continued his crowd-rousing motivation.

Finally, the moment had arrived. . . .

"Five, four, three, two, one—Happy New Year!" Every voice up in the party cheered, while the earsplitting siren sound of the party favors hypered the high energy that already filled the room.

Mel, Durty, Jay, Speedy, Chico, and me shook up our individual bottles of Moët and exploded them into the air, then showed some brotherly love amongst each other, while couples kissed and friends swapped hugs.

Following the welcoming of the new year, the DJ blasted Montel Jordan's back-in-the-day hit, "This Is How We Do It," and just about everyone rushed onto the dance floor singing the lyrics. The crowd moved nonstop as the DJs continued to heat up the party with the hottest jams, so it didn't take long before the various scents of perfume and cologne mixed with sweat and started to funk up the air.

Meanwhile, I glanced at Enychi still standing by the bar like she wasn't having a good time. And it looked like she was getting her drink on, too. As I checked up on Enychi inconspicuously throughout the night, I noticed her constantly tossing the cups up to her mouth. That's when I took Latavia by the hand and walked over towards the bar were Enychi was now leaning, instead of standing. My desire to make Enychi jealous turned into a real concern for her well-being.

"Ms. Aubrey, how many drinks did Denita's friend have?" I asked Mel's moms, who was a bit toasty herself.

"Too many to count, for somebody that said she don't drink. Now, shh! Don't mess up my count." Ms. Aubrey's voice slurred as she placed a stack of dollar bills in her bra and started another count from the overflowing jar of tips.

The party finally wound down and the crowd started to get smaller. Latavia didn't act like she was ready to call it a night.

Pressing her body against mines, she stood on her toes and whispered softly towards my ear, "Yo, I gotta go to the bathroom, but when I come back, I wanna get up outta this piece and go somewhere were we can start a little private party of our own, a'ight?" Latavia licked the side of my neck with her long, wet tongue and then excused herself for a moment to use the ladies' room.

I was attracted to Latavia's physical appearance, but a challenge is what really turns me on, and the way she had just threw the pussy at me and backed that ass up on the dance floor, I knew Latavia wasn't down to give me much of a struggle.

While she was in the rest room, I took a walk around the party, and then the lobby, to look for Denita, hoping that she hadn't had too much to drink and could make sure Enychi got home safely. Mel had disappeared hours ago, but that was no surprise, because I knew that nigga was going make sure he put that suite to use. By the time I made my way back into the ballroom, Enychi was gone, Ms. Aubrey looked like she was trying to holla at the DJ as he packed up his records, and Latavia was heading towards me.

"You ready, boo?" she said.

"Nah, hold up a minute. You seen where that girl went that was at the bar?"

"Why? Who's homegirl to you, yo, 'cause you was watching that bitch all night, dawg?" Latavia's whole demeanor changed, she had the ghetto, rolling motion of her head, and her fingers was in my face.

"Yo, shorty, that's my li'l sis Denita's friend, and if she had too much to drink, I just wanna make sure she get home safe, just like I would any female that was intoxicated. A'ight, so please. The attitude ain't necessary. Did you see where she went or no?" I lied, but so what? She wasn't gon' tell me otherwise.

"I don't know where she went. Some guy came up to her and she walked off with him."

"What? Yo, please, can you just wait here for a minute?" I had a bad gut feeling about that. My first instinct told me to go check Mel's room to see if maybe Denita and Enychi crashed in the extra bedroom, so that's what I had to do.

"Yo, hold up, son. You saying want me to wait here while you go check on another bitch? Nah, fuck that. I'm outta here." Latavia started walking away from me.

"A'ight then. It ain't like that, though, but I ain't about to stand here and argue with you. Latavia, just wait! Come with me." I grabbed her hand and rushed towards the elevator.

When I reached the top floor, my heart pounded as I hurried to the room. *Knock, knock, knock.* "Yo, Mel, it's Wa. Open up. Come on nigga. Hurry up."

"Yo, dawg, take it easy." Mel opened the door in his boxer shorts. "I was wondering when your ass was gonna come up and join the after party. Nigga, I am fucked up. Damn, she fine as hell. You can come on in, love." Mel signaled for Latavia to come in from the hallway.

"Yo, Mel, just close the door for a minute. She good," I demanded.

"Oh, it's like that? A'ight. Sweetheart, he'll be out in a minute—okay?" Mel said, before shutting the door.

I didn't wait to ask questions, I just walked straight into the bedroom Mel was sleeping in first. And in the bathroom I saw the twins Shakai and Shakima, and some other chick I didn't know, sitting in the small-size Jacuzzi, but I ain't see no Enychi.

"Yo, Mel, where your sister at?" I asked as I walked from the bedroom.

"Man, I don't know. Wherever she at, she grown. But, yo, what's up with shorty? Why you leave her out in the hall?" Mel inquired, drooling at the mouth all over again.

"Yo, I ain't feeling that chick like that. You seen Enychi?"

"Yo, nigga, I ain't seen nobody but them three bitches I got back there in the bathtub. But hold up. You said you ain't feeling shorty?"

"Nah, not really. Who in the other room?"

"That nigga Jay, and I think one of his boys, but I don't know who them niggas is with. But wait—since you ain't feeling homegirl, I could holla at her?"

I ain't never seen Mel act so thirsty over a chick before. He must've wanted Latavia bad. So I told him to handle his business, because my main concern was Enychi and where she could have disappeared to. Without knocking, I burst into the other bedroom, and just like I thought, that dusty-ass nigga Jay and a dude I ain't even know were in there, taking leftover bottles of Moët to the head, as they cracked jokes on the pink-flowered cotton drawers Enychi had on—while obviously trying to get in 'em. She was passed out, lying limp on the bed, with one arm dangling to the side. Her black slacks had been pulled down to the middle of her thighs.

"Yo, get the fuck off of her! What the fuck is wrong with y'all niggas?" I rushed over to Enychi. She was knocked out.

"Yo, Jay, you a foul ass. That's some fucked-up shit y'all niggas trying to do to this girl!"

"Yo, fuck you nigga," Jay said as he and his friend left the room.

I was mad as hell at them niggas, but mainly at Enychi's ass for getting this way. I couldn't understand why she would get herself so drunk. I was just glad I walked up in there when I did. After I managed to get her pants back up, I went to the bathroom and got a wet washcloth and wiped off her face, hoping that would get her to wake up, so I could take her home. Enychi was out of it, but the cold water got up her up enough to move her legs so I could walk her to my car.

"Hey, Wasuan." Enychi's voice slurred as she tried to talk. "Why you invite that girl, huh? When you know you like me?" Once I got her outside, she threw her arms around my neck and looked me in my face as I tried to get her inside the car. "It's okay, though. I was mad at you, but I ain't mad at you no more. And I'ma tell you a secret." Enychi put her mouth to my ear and whispered, "I like you, too—but I think I'm gonna be sick." I pulled her arms from around my neck, pushed her all the way in the seat, and fastened her seat belt. The thought of her liking me put a smile on my face. It's just too bad that she was drunk out of her mind when she said that.

Only, as I got in the driver's side, I remembered something my pops use to say: "The truth always comes out when you're drunk. Alcohol don't do nothing but give you the courage to do and say the shit you too scare to do and say when you're sober." As proof of that truth Enychi wasn't lying when she said she was gonna be sick—because, just as I pulled off, she started vomiting all over herself, me, and my car.

. . .

New Year's morning, I walked in holding Enychi's clothes nicely folded in the crook of my right arm.

"Enychi," I called out when I didn't see her lying in the bed anymore. For a moment I was scared she left and went home in just my T-shirt, but then I saw her shadow on the wall behind the door. Slowly, Enychi stepped out with a look of shame and embarrassment on her face, and I'm sure it was because I had seen her make a fool of herself last night. I also seen a slight sigh of relief come over Enychi when she saw that I wasn't a stranger. Of course, she didn't say anything. I know she had to be wondering what kind of impression I had of her now.

"Well, well, well. I see the alcoholic has arisen," I teased. "Here. Take your clothes. I washed them."

"Wait a minute, what do you mean 'washed them'? How did they get dirty and how did I get here?" Enychi questioned like she really didn't have a clue, so I took the opportunity to give her ass one.

"Oh, so, you mean to tell me you don't remember getting so fuckin' wasted last night that two niggas almost raped you, and that the reason I had to bring your drunk ass here to my place was because you was too fucked-up to tell me where you lived at? And I won't even mention all the fuckin' throw-up. I just came from cleaning out my car, right before I went to the laundry to wash out your nasty clothes and mines because you can't hold your liquor. So, is there any more questions, Lucy the Lush?" I was vexed with Enychi for conducting herself in such a reckless manner.

"Ha, ha, ha. Very funny. Well, thank you, but I do have another question." Enychi looked everywhere but at me. "Did we have sex last night?" she asked.

"What? Come on now. Contrary to what you might think about me, that ain't how I get down. Besides, I don't know what you're used to, but if I did run up in it, you would've felt it, woke up, and remembered it. A nigga might be skinny, but don't sleep on what's packed away in these jeans, mama." I had to let her ass know just for the record.

Enychi sighed. "Well, I'm glad about that. I mean the part about, nothing happening; but you could've kept the rest of that information to yourself. Now, can I use your bathroom so I can get dressed and you can take me home?"

"Yeah, you can. But let me ask you something first."

Enychi cut her eyes at me and slightly turned up her lips, showing off that ungrateful-ass attitude of hers again. "Go ahead, but make it quick," she said.

"A'ight: What that hell were you thinking last night?" I asked, raising my voice.

"What? I don't know who the hell you think you're talking to like that. I don't have to answer to you."

"Yeah, you're right. You don't. But the next time you're out somewhere and the drinks just happen to sneak up on you, you might not be so lucky to run across a nigga like me that's gonna look out for your ass. The bathroom is at the end of the hall to your left." I was mad as hell at her, and called myself dismissing her.

Enychi got an embarrassed look on her face again. "Wait, hold up a minute. I know I might've had a little too much to drink last night, but I'm not a drinker, so I don't make getting drunk a habit, okay!" Enychi spoke defensively.

"Oh, you don't? Well, that's good to know, 'cause last night you could've fooled the hell out of me!"

"What is your problem? I mean what's up with all your nasty remarks?" Enychi leaned herself up against the bedroom door with her arms folded and waited for my response.

"My problem is the fact that you come off like you're so fucking high and mighty, with that nasty-ass attitude of yours, but then you go and get drunk, carry your ass up to the room with a nigga you don't know and shit, so him and his boy could hit it—but you give a nigga like me—that really cares about you—a hard time. What's up with that?"

"Look, Wasuan, I really can't comment on last night, because I don't remember what happened. And if what you said is true, then thank you. But as far as you caring about me, I can't tell. Especially since you and your little girlfriend looked like such a happy couple."

"Oh, so, you remember that part? Did it bother you?" I asked, anticipating a yes from her.

Eynchi looked down at the floor. "No! Why should it?"

"Stop frontin'." I walked up and stood about three inches from her. "You know you want me. You told me you did last night," I said, in a suave but seductive tone that had Enychi fidgeting.

"Get out my way!" she yelled, ignoring my claim. Pushing me out her way, Enychi stomped down the hallway and into the bathroom.

I give up, I said to myself throwing my hands in the air. I wanted to be through with Enychi, because I couldn't figure her out for the life of me. And yet, call me crazy, but that's what I liked about her.

After she got dressed I drove her ass home. But I spent the next couple of nights falling asleep with the scent of her in my bed sheets, filling my nose.

W A S U A N

I hadn't seen Enychi since she moved out almost a month ago, but she finally responded to the message I left on her cell phone voice mail two weeks ago—about some mail she had over here.

She called and asked if it was okay if she stopped by to pick it up. I was nervous as hell, but looking forward to seeing her face again.

The crib was a mess. I had clothes scattered all over the living room. I hadn't washed the sheets or made the bed since she left. The kitchen sink was full of dirty dishes, and the floor needed a good mopping. I couldn't let Enychi come over and see the place looking like that.

After two hours of cleaning, I sat on the couch, popped open a cold Heineken, watched a karate flick, and waited for Enychi. About an hour into the movie, I started dozing off.

The blare of the buzzer caused me to jump out of my sleep. "Yeah," I said into the intercom.

"It's Enychi." The sound of her soft voice got my dick hard. I buzzed her in the downstairs door.

I stood by the door, impatiently waiting for her to get off the elevator and ring the bell.

When she did, I stared at her through the peephole—just for a few seconds. And, damn, she still looked good. I knew I missed her, but I ain't realize how much I was missing her until I saw her.

"Hey!" I spoke very casually as I opened the door—and I walked away before she could walk inside. As I sat back down in front of the TV, Enychi came on in.

"Hi," she responded dryly with an *okay now, gimme my mail* look written all over her face.

The smell of her sweet-ass perfume was torture. I flagged my hand in the direction of the dining area. "Your mail is on the table."

"Thanks. Hopefully, this is the last of it, because I did an address change almost two weeks ago."

"Yo, it's all good, unless you can't handle seeing me." I just said that to get a reaction and feel her out.

"I can handle seeing you. It's not easy, but I can handle it."

"Umm, I hear that."

"Well, I'ma go now. Thanks again," Enychi said, reaching for the knob on the door.

"Yo, can I talk to you for a minute?"

"Wasuan, I just came—"

I cut her off midsentence. "Please, one minute, that's all."

Enychi exhaled deeply and gave me a funny look. "Okay, but only one minute, Wasuan."

"A'ight. So how you doing?" I asked her.

"I'm good."

"And school? That good, too?"

"Yes."

"Yeah, you about to be done with that, right?"

"Yeah. In a couple of weeks, I graduate."

"Wow, that's great. Maybe you'll let me take you out to dinner or something—you know, to celebrate."

Enychi sucked her teeth and folded her arms across her chest. "Wasuan, come on."

"Come on what? I'm serious."

"Well, I can't!"

"Oh, so it's like that now!" I started to get upset.

"Look, I gotta go!" Enychi rushed out into the hallway. I followed behind her as she pressed on the elevator button about ten times.

"Yo, Enychi. Wait, please! I really miss you and, yo, man, I'm sorry for doing that stupid shit I did. Please, just chill with me for a little while—that's all I'm asking."

"I can't. Wasuan. I can't." Enychi's eyes started to tear up and so did mines. I took that as an opportunity to comfort her, in hopes that she'd reciprocate; but as I tried to hold her, she stepped back from me like I was contagious. "No, Wasuan. Stop, don't do this."

"Nych, come on. I know you still love me just as much as I love you. I fucked up big time and I know that. Baby girl, I'll change for you, I promise. Just come back to me, please. I'm not complete without you. I need you, ma." Even though Enychi refused to look at me I knew she still loved me. Her emotions told it all. I walked closer to her, and this time she showed no sign of resistance.

I took her in my arms and softly kissed her on her forehead, cheeks, and then her lips—when, suddenly, the damn elevator doors opened and fucked up everything. Enychi broke away from my arms and made her way onto the elevator.

"I'm sorry Wasuan, but I'm happy with Tone," she said as the doors closed shut. Damn. Enychi might as well have just stabbed me in the heart, because that shit probably wouldn't have hurt as much as the words that had just come out of her mouth.

After spending days feeling depressed and being cooped up in the house since Enychi dropped that bomb on me, I got a call from Mel.

"Yo, what up, Wa? You still living, or what, man? I know you ain't still trippin' over ol girl, 'cause, dawg, you gotta let homegirl go, man. Come out and chill, nigga," he said.

"Nah, I don't feel like it."

"Fuck her, dawg. It's more pussy out in the sea," Mel hollered in the cell phone as he tried to get me out of my funk.

"Mel, I'm good."

"Nigga, you ain't good. Bring ya ass out the house. Matter of fact, I'm coming to get you, man."

"Nah, nigga, chill. I'm a'ight.'

"Yeah, a'ight, be alright. But I'm still on my way over to get you out that crib." Mel ended the call before I could refuse him again. I knew his ass was serious about getting me up on outta here, so I got up off the couch and went into the shower.

By the time I put on my clothes, Mel was ringing my cell phone to let me know he was downstairs.

I grabbed my coat and left out the apartment, then it dawned on me that a nigga needed a haircut badly, so I ran back in the crib and got my blue Yankees fitted cap.

Mel was parked out in front of my building, blasting his music as usual.

"What up, homie?" Mel said as soon as I got in his ride.

"I'm chilling, nigga."

"Yeah, I heard you, cuz." Mel wasn't buying my shit, though.

"Yo, man. I need a fuckin' haircut. Take me to the barber shop."

"Come on, nigga, that shit be crowded as hell on a fuckin' Saturday."

"So what, nigga? You ain't doing shit."

"What? Nigga, my time is money. Shit, I got shit to do when I don't got shit to do," Mel argued.

"Yeah, a'ight, well drop me off and then come scoop me when I'm done," I told him.

"A'ight, I could do that."

"So, what up with 'Nita's ass?"

"She a'ight, doing her, you know, that."

"Um, what about Enychi? She been around?"

"Nah, but I heard she running that nigga Tone's store now."

"I hear that. I told you she told me, she was in happy being with that nigga, right?"

"Nigga, yes, you told me that about ten times already."

"Ahh, nigga, fuck you. I know I ain't said that shit that many times!" I had to laugh at that bullshit, 'cause I knew I didn't tell that to this nigga that many times.

"Listen, after you get your shit lined the fuck up, I'ma take your ass to the strip club and get a few of them chicks to push up on you so you can block that bitch Enychi out your mutha-fuckin' mind, nigga!"

"Yo, it ain't that serious, dawg. Besides, them chicks be a'ight to look at, but I don't want their sweaty-ass asses up on me like that. That shit don't even do nothing for me."

"That's 'cause you concentrating too hard on their asses being sweaty, instead of just enjoying all that ass rubbing up on you." Mel laughed.

"Nah, I just ain't with that shit, that's all."

"A'ight, but you need to find you another bitch from somewhere to lift them muthafuckin' spirits of yours, dawg. Yo, what happened to that bad-ass bitch—the light-skinned chick from Baisley? Yo, word up, I ain't gon' lie; I tried to get with her ass hard that night, but she wasn't tryna hear that shit, man."

"*Latavia?* Word? I thought you hit it."

"I tried like hell, but she wasn't feeling me, dawg," Mel admitted.

"Man, I ain't talk to that girl in about two years. She probably got a man or a kid by now."

"So what? It won't hurt to holla at the broad and see what's up."

"Yeah, I still got her number, too."

"Well, there it is. Now get out of my whip and go get your shit done up." Mel slowed up in front of the barber shop.

"Yo', it ain't nobody in Rob's chair right now, so come back for me in twenty minutes, nigga," I told Mel as I hopped out his car and looked through the shop's window.

"A'ight, in twenty I'll be back," Mel claimed.

"I'm serious, Mel. Don't have a nigga waiting."

"Yo, dawg, twenty minutes. I got you," he said as he sped off.

I walked inside the barber shop, said "What's up?" to everybody, and sat in my man's chair.

As he started cutting my hair, I thought about what Mel said, about giving Latavia a call. I searched through my phone for her number, but before I pressed the button to dial her I thought back to the last time I saw her, to make sure I wasn't a complete asshole.

"Hello," she answered, sounding sexy as hell.

"Is this Latavia?"

"Why, who's this?" she said.

"It's Wasuan, I met—"

"Yeah, yeah, yeah, I remember who you are. What you want?"

"Damn, I gotta want something to call you?"

"Yeah! You ain't been calling me."

"I know, but you cross my mind all the time. Today, I got up enough courage to call and see how you were doing."

"Umm, okay!"

"That's all you gon' say? If so, I'm not sure I'm feeling the way this conversation is going down."

"Well, considering how things went down between us, you should be feeling the fact that you're getting some conversation and not the dial tone," she said.

"Yeah, you're right. Did you get married yet?" I asked, thinking it would be in my best interest to change the subject.

"Excuse me?"

"Did you get married yet?"

"No, not yet." I could tell she was smiling.

"Why is that? You was waiting for me?"

"What? You funny," she laughed.

"Nah, I'm serious. I need to see you!"

"Wasuan. After two years, what makes you wanna see me now?" she asked in her soft, ghetto-girl inflection.

"I don't know, besides missing you. I guess a nigga finally came to his senses. So, listen. Can I take you out?"

"Oh my God, Wasuan," she giggled. "You had me at hello. Nah, I'm just playing. For real though, I'm feeling real crazy about this, but a'ight, I guess you can take me out to eat or sumthin'."

"A'ight, that'll work. You still live in Baisley, right?"

"No, I been moved. I live in them buildings on Merrick and 109."

"A'ight. I know where that is. So, I can see you tonight, around eight?"

"Yeah, that's cool."

I flipped my cell phone shut and was feeling better already.

Just as my barber was brushing the loose hairs from the back of my head and neck, Mel was pulling up to the front of the store front. *His timing couldn't have been better.* Twenty minutes, just like he said. I paid Rob, and just as I was walking towards the door Tone walked in.

Purposely brushing past me, he bumped my shoulder and gave me this smart-ass smirk.

Fuck him and Enychi, I thought to myself, as I left the barber shop.

"Yo, I saw that nigga Tone walk up in there. You cool?" Mel asked holding his gun in his lap when I climbed in the car.

I waved my hand in dismissal. "Yeah, I'm cool. Fuck that nigga." That shit wasn't even worth going into detail about. "Yo, I called shorty. We hookin' up tonight, so you can slide me back to the crib." I said, switching the subject.

138

"For real, or you just saying that so I won't take your ass to the tittie bar?" Mel laughed.

"Nah, yo, shorty really letting me take her out." I smiled.

"A'ight. That's what's up. That's what I'm talking about, keep it moving, playboy."

ENYCHI

I was planning a romantic dinner for me and Tone, since my new apartment finally felt like home, now that we had finished painting and furnishing the place.

My color scheme of warm forest green, crème de menthe, and pumpkin orange, along with Tone's impeccable taste in furniture, had the apartment looking like something from outta *House Beautiful* magazine. It was simply beautiful.

Actually, so was our relationship. Tone spent plenty of time with me, so the fact that he was married didn't bother me at all. As a matter of fact, I was convinced that there was nothing going on between them, just like he said. But when I heard him on the phone, telling his little girls how much he loved them, I felt like a piece of shit. I'd gone into this with my eyes wide open, but at times like that, no matter what Tone said, I felt like I was coming in between him and his family.

It helped that Tone showed so much interest in me. Especially on the few nights he did go home to be with his kids. Tone would call me at least three times, just to tell me how much he was missing me. He knew how to make a girl feel like his number one, and that always scored him some cool points.

I felt as though our situation was finally developing into something special, which meant my feelings for Wasuan would eventually fade. *I was in a better place, being with Tone, anyway,* I told myself as I was entering the bank to deposit a little something towards safekeeping.

"Hey, baby," I answered my cell phone with a cheesy smile spread across my face, as I was leaving the supermarket.

"You answer your phone like that for everybody?" Tone questioned playfully.

"Only for you, baby."

"I'm starting to feel like you got a whole lotta game with you, ma." He laughed. "Anyway, what you doing?"

"I'm just leaving the grocery store. Baby, I'm gonna cook you a meal so good that it's gonna make you call your wife and tell her to kiss the kids, 'cause you ain't coming home no more," I teased.

"Oh, word? I'm looking forward to that, but I'ma need you to put that meal on hold for me."

"Why, 'cause you ain't trying to leave her?" I got upset real quick, because, here I was trying to do something nice for him and he says to put it on hold.

"Yo, why you tryna start something? I said that 'cause I want you to go home and pack a small bag."

"For what?"

"We're going on a trip."

"Where're we going?"

"Does it matter? You're going with me and we'll be back in time for your final exams."

"Yes, it matters. I need to know what to pack."

"Pack some underclothes and your toiletries. You can get clothes when we get to where we're going."

I wondered what Tone was up to. "All right," I said. My hostility turned back into excitement as I rushed home to pack.

Three hours later we were sitting in first-class on a runway at LaGuardia waiting to take off to the Bahamas. I didn't even have a clue to where we was going, until we got to the ticket counter. While we were taxiing down the runway, I turned to Tone and asked "How come you didn't say we were going to the Bahamas?"

"I really wanted to take you somewhere else, like Turks and Caicos, or Southern France, to get your mind off this bullshit for these last couple of days, so you can get ready for your graduation. I figured you'd already been to the Bahamas before. But since I came up with the idea this morning, it was easier to get a flight to the Bahamas. And I have a house there."

"You do?" I asked, trying to mask some of the excitement in my voice. I'd seen the likes of cash when I was with Wa, but the way this nigga Tone was dropping it on me was unbelievable!

"Yeah, I got me a nice li'l spot."

"I didn't know that."

"There's a lot you don't know about me."

"I'm finding that out more and more each day," I said.

"Don't start wit the slick shit, please," Tone warned.

Rolling my eyes, I told him, "That's your guilt making you take it the wrong way. What I meant was, the more time we spend together the more you open up to me. I'm beginning to see a side of you that I didn't know exists."

"What do you mean?" Curiosity was written all over his face.

"You know, you always give off this thugged-out persona. When in reality you're caring, intelligent, and cultured."

"Enychi, I hate having to keep my game face on all the time. I'm never faking, you know what, it's like where we come from, it is a part of who I am. Sometimes—actually a lot of times—I like to relax and be me. But niggas in the street would mistake that type of shit for weakness. So, the only time I get to be laid back is when I'm spending time with my kids or with you."

"Damn, I never thought about it that way."

Tone leaned over and planted a nice, soft kiss on my lips. "These next few days you're going to see a lot of the real me."

Wow, this should be very interesting, I thought, as the plane soared into the air.

Tone saying he had a nice li'l spot was definitely an understatement. This nigga had a beautiful ranch-style home. The outside was painted pale peach, which I thought was great for an island home. It would've of looked ridiculous in the middle of Queens, but here it was perfect. The outside was nothing, compared to what I saw when we crossed the threshold. My God, I felt like I stepped into the summer home edition of *Better Homes and Gardens* magazine. I ran from room to room like an elated child. Each of the six rooms were painted a different bright color, with the perfect complimenting furniture.

After I finished taking in the house, I found Tone at the bar in his den mixing drinks.

143

"You don't waste no time, do you?" I teased.

"This?" he said, smiling, holding up the bottles of Hypnotiq and Armandale. "This is to set off the relaxation."

"Uhh-huh." I smirked. "I love this house. It's beautiful."

"Thanks."

"Your wife did an excellent job of decorating." My comment was drenched in sarcasm.

But, with a little chuckle, Tone told me, "My wife don't even know this house exist."

"She doesn't?" I said, slightly embarrassed for talking too soon.

"Nah, so wipe the egg off your face, ma. Only people that been up in here is my parents, one of my boys, and now you." Tone handed me a drink and sat down next to me. "This is where I come to when I want to get away from everything. It's real peaceful here, no stress. I would like to keep it that way," he said, staring right into my eyes. I nodded my head in agreement and decided to put my sarcastic mouth away for the remainder of the vacation.

"Wake up. You tryna to sleep the day away or something?" Tone said, shaking me.

"Yes," I said, curling my nude body up even tighter beneath the extremely soft sheets. "I need a lot of sleep after that workout you put me through last night."

"Shit, I was tired last night, wait 'til tonight."

"I'm afraid."

"Girl, get up and eat some of this food, so we can get out and do some things."

Opening my eyes I peeked at him and the food on the tray that he was holding. They both looked delicious. Tone was wearing a bright, white G-Unit wife-beater, a pair of khaki cargo shorts, and brown Vuitton flip-flops. His body looked so good, I was ready to pull him back into bed and ride him. I had to squeeze my legs together to stop my coochie from throbbing. I sat up smiling at him. I know I looked silly with my hair all over my head, and dried-up slob on my face.

Tone sat the tray on my lap, then leaned over and kissed my lips. "Good morning, chocolate sunshine."

"Good morning to you." I glanced down at the tray, then up at him. "Now, there is no way you cooked this food."

"You right. Bev cooked it."

"Who is Bev?" I asked, trying to keep the sheet over my bare breasts while I nibbled at a piece of French toast.

"She's sort of like a maid, but I don't like to call her that. Bev watches over the house for most of the year. When I'm here she cooks and cleans for me."

"So, what we getting into today?"

"We gonna do some shopping, and whatever else makes you happy."

"Really?"

"Yes, really." Reading the joyful expression plastered all over my face, he said "You seem really excited about that."

"You were right, I have been to the Bahamas before. I went with Wasuan on a cruise. I know, you don't wanna hear about him, and I'm not trying to talk about him. Let me just say this, when I came here with him I was bored out of my mind. All he did the entire trip was stay on the ship, in the casino, gambling."

Tone simply shook his head. "I'ma make you forget all about that trip, ma. Okay?"

"Okay." I smiled.

Shopping with Tone that day was like giving a little kid fifty dollars and turning them loose in a candy store. The first place we stopped in was a fabric store. It was full of beautiful colors, exotic prints, and textures I knew I would never find back home. I didn't mean to go crazy in there, but I came up with the perfect design for every pattern that caught my eye. Tone had to drop at least thirty-five hundred on me in that store. Next, we hit the Gucci store, and I picked up the cutest pair of gold-and-pink, metal-framed sunglasses, and a pink handbag to match.

We strolled through a few more high-end stores and Tone continued to spend cash. Finally, we spotted my favorite store, Prada. I saw so many bags and shoes that I had to have! Tone watched as I pranced around trying on shoe after shoe, holding up bag after bag.

"Okay, baby, I need you to help me choose."

"Get whichever ones you want, baby girl," he said nonchalantly, like money was not an issue at all.

"Come on, I want you to help me pick two bags and two pairs of shoes."

"If you like all that, just get it."

The saleslady's little pale face lit up. "I think you should listen to him," she said.

Yeah, I bet you do. I cut my eyes at her as I remembered my manners, and said, "Could you excuse us for a moment, please?"

"No problem. Take as much time as you need," she responded.

When she was out of earshot, I turned to Tone and said, "This is about twelve thousand dollars worth of stuff, Tone. I can't let you spend that kind of money in here. You've already spent crazy dough on me today."

He gave me this *are you serious* look and said, "'Let me spend'? Yo, you know how many girls would be jumping through hoops to be in the position you're in right now? You bugging the fuck out!"

"Hold the fuck up, Tone. First of all, I'm not like them many chicks you talking about. Of course I like the way you drop paper on me, but I learned from my situation with Wasuan that this shit don't last forever." I took a deep breath. "That's why, when we get to New York I'm going to start looking for a job."

"Enychi, are you getting that shit or what?" he asked like he hadn't heard a word I said.

"Tone, was you even listening to a word I said?"

"Yeah, I heard you. You want to get a job. I got the perfect job for you. I need a new store manager, someone that can help me upgrade the store's image. And, since you go to school for fashion, you think you can help me with that?"

"Sure I can help you with that, but what happens if we stop seeing each other? Do I lose my job?"

"Nah, but you're 'bout to graduate, soon."

"And?"

"I'll help you open your own store and put everything in your name. That'll be my graduation gift to you. Then you won't have to depend on me or any other nigga. Is that cool with you?"

Hell, yeah, I was cool with that. That's exactly what I wanted. But I didn't dare let him see my excitement. I simply answered, "I guess so."

"A'ight. Now call that bitch back over so I can pay for that stuff and we can get up outta here. I'm hungrier than a hostage." He managed to rub on his stomach while holding my many shopping bags in his hands.

I had so many bags, I didn't know how we would get back through customs.

Since Tone's place was a bit of a distance from Paradise Island, we got a room at the Royal Towers so we could leave the bags there, freshen up, and go get something to eat. The hotel room was colorful, with tropical decor features, matching bedspread and drapes that displayed a coral motif in blue, green, and orange, along with light-colored furniture that accented the room just right. I dropped my bags, rushed over to the balcony, and, as I stepped out on it, I fell in love with the Atlantic Ocean view. I knew exactly why they called this Paradise Island, because it was the most beautiful place I ever saw.

Later, we sipped margaritas, ate stuffed lobster, and fed each other dessert, at a restaurant in the hotel called Fathoms. After lunch, we checked out the aquariums, avoided the casinos—and I couldn't wait to hit the beach. The white sands, the clear azure waters, the palm trees, and the cloudless sky, were such a pleasant sight to see as we laid next to one another in a hammock.

Tone's body was amazingly buff and in shape for thirty-five. I watched through the darkness of my shades as women walked by and clocked Tone, like they'd fuck him in a heartbeat if I turned my back.

"Baby," I said to him, "I see you got a lot of fans checking you out. I'm almost scared to leave your side!" I smiled, but I was dead serious.

"Well, you ain't gotta be scared. I'm loving what I got right here, mama." Tone kissed me, and I got up and grabbed his hand, pulling him out of his chair so we could hit the ocean. "Yo, you looking real sexy in that bikini," Tone complimented the Salvatore Ferragamo two-piece bathing suit he bought me, as we splashed around in the blue waters.

"Thanks baby, I really feel special."

"I told you I got you, ma. You just gotta trust in me."

As the sun began to go down we enjoyed the view of it as we strolled the beach.

"*Uwe, la, la, we, we,*" a Bahamian man said as he passed us by, balancing a tray full of frozen drinks on top of his head.

"Yeah, you like that, don't you? Too bad that's all mine," Tone teased, shaking his head at the guy. It was good to see that he could handle another man complimenting me without any jealousy.

"Let me take some pictures of you," Tone smiled, turning on the digital camera that was strapped around his shoulder. I leaned against a cove near the far end of the beach and smiled for the camera.

"Take off your clothes," he instructed with a sexy grin on his face.

I wasn't sure if he was kidding or not, but the more he

snapped my picture, the more aroused I started to get. Talk about a turn-on, we made love on the sand as the sun set. And of course we didn't care who saw us.

Our five-day vacation was filled with plenty of sex, dips in the ocean, shopping, dancing until the wee hours of the morning, and falling asleep, cuddling at night to the sound of the ocean lapping gently outside this cozy home.

ENYCHI

A week after we returned to New York, as Tone promised, I took over managerial duties at his store. My new position was great, although it seemed to be met with some resistance from two of his female employees, Alicia and Kiki. I couldn't understand why at first, then I found out that they both were good friends with the former store manager, some bitch named Tasheka. The first couple of days, they played little games with me, like taking long breaks, doing their assigned task whenever they felt like it, or just plain not doing nothing at all. So, during one of the new biweekly, required staff meetings that I implemented, I laid down the rules very firmly.

Right before the end of the meeting in front of the store's eight employees, I let it be known, looking directly at Alicia and Kiki, that "I will not tolerate disrespectful attitudes. If you cannot follow my instructions when given, you know where the door is. Any time you feel you wanna come from break when you get good and ready, you will be written up and your pay will be docked. If you get wrote up twice for any reason, you will be suspended for one week. The third time that you are written up you will be automatically terminated. Am I making myself clear?" I asked this, still staring at the pair. From the corners of my eyes I could see that the other employees immediately nodded in agreement, but those two bitches had delayed responses. "If not, again, there's the door, you can kindly take this time to leave the store and never return. Meeting adjourned." I turned and headed towards the office.

Kiki must've thought I was out of earshot, 'cause I heard her say in a low voice, "Who that bitch think she is?"

I stopped in my tracks and turned around to let her know in a professional manner, exactly who I was. "Excuse me, I'm your boss. And since you need some kind of confirmation for that, look on the bottom of the slip at my signature when I finish writing you up."

She just stood there with her mouth open, like she was stuck on stupid. I just got through telling those little 'hood rats I wasn't there to play games with them, yet she had to try me. After that day I didn't have any more real problems from them, or any of the other employees, for that matter.

My life outside of the store was pretty decent. I passed all of my exams with As. I even used some of the fabrics I got from the Bahamas for my final sewing projects. My professors were impressed by my designs, but my choice of fabrics blew them away. Needless to say, graduation was in the bag.

In my free time I worked on getting my business started. I decided to open a small boutique in Manhattan, where I could sell high-end brands and my own designs. I even enlisted Denita's help, since she wasn't doing shit but hopping from one part-time internship to the next, or gossiping with her mother about who did what with who in the projects, on a daily basis.

Everything was coming along better than I imagined. Tone's realtor found me a reasonably priced storefront. I hired one of my friends from school, who majored in interior design, to decorate the store. All of my paperwork was in order and all the brands I wanted to carry were willing to distribute to me. Only thing I didn't have yet was a name.

When I wasn't running Tone's store or planning the opening of mine, I was with Tone. How could I not view him as *my* man? He stayed at my house every night, and if he did decide to go home it was at three or four in the morning.

Just like that, Tone had become my ghetto knight in blinging armor. On Sunday, my day off, he called me up and told me, "Get dressed I need you to come scoop me from the Benz dealer. I had to bring my car in, something's wrong with my engine."

Happily, I agreed, "Sure, baby." Although Sundays was the only day I got to sleep late, I got up, took a quick shower, threw on a Juicy sweatsuit, and was out the door in fifteen minutes.

When I pulled up to the lot, the first thing I saw was Tone motioning for me to get out the car. *Why the hell do I have to get out?* I got out and walked over to where he was standing, chatting with one of the car salesmen. He stopped talking long enough to give me a quick hug and kiss, then he introduced me to guy, "Enychi, this is Big Paulie the owner. Paulie, this is my lady, Enychi."

The heavyset Italian man extended his hand to me, "It's nice to meet you, Enychi."

"It's nice to meet you, too, Paulie," I said, shaking his extremely soft, manicured hand.

Paulie turned to Tone. "Let me know when you're ready. You know I always give you the best deals."

"A'ight, Paulie." Tone turned back to me. "You got all the papers for your car?"

"Yeah, why?"

"Cause you 'bout to trade it in. Get you something fresh."

"But, ain't nothing wrong with my car, though!"

"Yeah, well, everytime I look at it I think about that faggot-ass nigga, Wasuan. I can't have my lady riding around in a car that some bum-ass nigga ain't even pay in full for."

"Exactly, so how how can I trade it in, when I still have payments to make?"

"Let me worry about that," Tone said with a sly smile.

An hour and a half later, I pulled off the lot in a white SL55. Man, you know I was really feeling myself then. That night I had to put it down on Tone's ass for sure. I sucked and slurped on his dick until my lips started to swell. The nigga bought me a hundred-thousand-dollar whip! For that, I fucked him so long his dick started to hurt.

Only, life wouldn't be life, without the necessary reality check every now and then. Please believe that that following Tuesday I received a nice one.

Around two that afternoon, Denita stopped by the store with papers I needed to sign in order to set up accounts with some of the clothing distributors. After I signed them we were standing around talking about nothing in particular, just being girls. While we were conversing, I kept my eye on this one chick that was browsing—she had real pretty golden brown skin, nice, long brown hair cut in layers, with honey blonde highlights. I couldn't tell whether she was Black or Dominican. Denita must've saw the way I was watching the chick, 'cause she said, "Nych, what's up with ol' girl?"

"I don't know, she keep looking over here, then looking away. I thought she might be trying to pull the fake pregnancy act, but that ain't no fake belly. Plus, she look too well kept to be stealing."

"You trippin', Nych. All boosters don't look like crackheads. They getting money."

Even if the girl wasn't a booster, something about her still made me uncomfortable. Then I noticed Alicia standing over in the corner. She thought I didn't see her watching me and the chick. When I looked back in the girl's direction, she was walking straight toward me with her arms filled with clothes. "I want you to add these up, bag 'em, and put them on my bill."

Denita and I exchanged quick glances, then looked back at the girl. Trying not to sound too sarcastic, I told her, "I'm sorry, miss, but we don't do bills here."

"It's Mrs., and I don't really need a bill. If I wanted to, I could just walk outta here with this shit in my hand."

"Now you trippin', homegirl. If you're going to purchase those items, please do so. If not, them put them back and leave."

"And if I do neither?"

This bitch is really trying my patience. "I'll call the police."

"Sorry, sweetheart, but you can't call the police on the owner."

"The owner?"

"Yes, honey. The owner and Tone's wife, *Natalie*. If you check all the licenses back there in your little office, they're in my name. Legally, all this is mine. Now, bag my shit so I can leave, thank you!"

Denita frowned up her face and interfered, "Don't nobody

care whose wife you is, bitch. Enychi is the manager here, and you need to respect that."

"I got this," I said, cutting Denita off, 'cause this was still Tone's wife and I didn't want to outright disrespect her, although she was doing a great job of disrespecting me.

Natalie laughed, directing her attention toward Denita. "So what she's the manager? She ain't the first one of his sluts he's had working up in here, and she won't be the last. I just ran his last whore, Tasheka, up outta here three months ago. As a matter of fact, after I give birth to our third child, I think I'll just come back and run *my* store the same way I run *our* house. So, I hope you don't have no wild ideas in your head about him leaving me to be with you, 'cause that'll never happen."

By now I was vexed—especially after I spotted Alicia staring hard, with a Kool Aid smile spread across her face. But I knew how to handle Tone's wife without stepping to far out of place. Looking her right in the eye, I said "Whatever you may think your husband is doing, you need to check him. Don't get me wrong, if my man never spent any time with me, stayed away from our house for days on end, and only came home in the wee morning hours, I'd be suspicious, too. Me, personally, I would deal with him, though. Also, you're more than welcome to come run your store right now, *sweetheart*. This was never a permanent job for me, since Tone assisted me in opening my own luxury boutique. So, let me grab my purse and I'll be out your way."

Denita cracked a devilish smile. "Now bag your own shit, bitch!" she said.

I grabbed my personal belongings and Denita and I got the

fuck outta there, leaving Natalie's pregnant ass standing right in the middle of the store looking stupid. The smile that Alicia was wearing minutes earlier was gone, and it took everything in me not to hawk and spit in her face on the way out. I wasn't worried about her, though. I had bigger fish to fry. I couldn't wait to talk to Tone's ass.

Outside of Tone's store, Denita went on for a good five minutes about how she felt I should've handled the situation. She said plain and simple, "So what if his wife is knocked up? Don't be mad. Just keep stacking that nigga's paper, girl."

Part of me felt like, *fuck it, Denita's right.* I hated to admit it, but this time around love ain't have shit to do with nothing. I cared a great deal about Tone, but that's where it ended. I waited for 'Nita to hop into her brother's hooptie, and together we pulled out, going our separate ways.

As I was driving, that *I don't give a shit* attitude started to fade. *I can't believe his wife is pregnant.*

I was crushed. How could Tone lie to me like that? She looked about five, or maybe six, months, so things between them couldn't possibly be as bad as he claimed they were.

And he told me to trust him. Hum, he got some nerve. Trust my ass! Hell, in less than two months, Tone's had a bad surprise to go with every good one! What a difference between him and Wasuan. At least I loved Wasuan, and I sure as hell didn't have to worry about a pregnant wife and some fucking kids.

I had fifteen grand in the bank, a brand new Benz, and my own boutique. I didn't have to put up with Tone's shit anymore.

It was definitely time I moved on, because I wasn't cut out for his kind of drama, after all.

While I was driving, I turned on the radio and, *Wow!* I

thought, as I flipped through the stations. Of all days, how strange was it for Jagged Edge's song, "He Can't Love You Like I Love You," to be playing on two stations when it had to be at least five years old. Automatically, Wasuan came to mind as I listened to the lyrics of the song; and I reminisced about how good things use to be between us. I knew it wasn't right, but I really missed him.

All I wanted to do was go home, watch Lifetime movies, sob, and pig out on fried chicken and pistachio ice cream from my favorite takeout place.

As I turned into the parking lot of New York Fried Chicken, I could have sworn that I saw Wasuan through the big front window of the restaurant. As I was about to park, I spotted his car, which confirmed it was him.

Oh my God! My heart started to pound rapidly. I pulled down the sun visor to check my hair and makeup in the mirror and both were fine. I could've placed my order at the drive-through, but I decided to park my ride right next to his, just to see if he'd notice me.

But as he was heading towards his car, I saw that Wasuan wasn't alone. I squinted my eyes to get a better look at the girl walking close behind, because she looked familiar. I knew I'd seen her somewhere before. Once she got up on the passenger side of Wasuan's car, it clicked: That was the girl he was with at Mel's party a couple of years back. If I hadn't had that run-in with Natalie, *and* found out that she was pregnant, I probably wouldn't have said a word. But the next thing I knew, I was steppin' out of my car, "Wasuan!" I yelled, ready to go off.

He looked at me with a cold stare and didn't say a word.

"So, I see you went back to that?" I look at the girl like she was a foul odor in the air.

Before Wasuan could respond, Ms. Thing did it for him, "Uhh-huh. Who the fuck is you?" she said.

"Never mind who I am, bitch." I stepped towards her. "How long y'all been seeing each other?" I could hear myself talking crazy, but I couldn't seem to stop myself. *Wasuan was seeing this girl all along*, I started to think.

Wasuan slid himself in between us. "Hold up, Enychi! Chill. Latavia, just get in the car. Don't say nothing, a'ight? Let me handle this."

"Let you handle this? What the fuck you mean, let you handle this? That was the problem, remember—you couldn't handle *this*! So, tell me, was it because of her, is she the reason you flipped? Is that it, Wasuan? Were you fucking her while you were with me?" I was buggin'.

Wasuan took a deep breath before he answered. "Nah, I wasn't. That was you. You was the one sneaking around and getting your fuck on, not me. But if I did, why would it matter now? A couple of weeks ago you ain't wanna hear shit I had to say. Now you see me with a friend and wanna trip? Go 'head with that shit. Besides, what happened to *I'm happy*? I see you fly now, hopping outta that nigga's Benz, working in his store, playing his sloppy seconds, and that nigga don't even give two shits about you. But, huh, if that's the kind of shit that makes you happy, then be happy, mama!"

Listening to Wasuan speak to me with such a blasé attitude bothered the hell out out of me, but I let him vent before I shut it down. "You know what? You're right. It don't even matter. So,

I apologize to you and your little 'hood-rat friend. And you know what else? I *might* be Tone's sloppy seconds, and *maybe* he don't give a shit about me, but with gifts like this—" I opened the door to my Benz and got back in it, "—who gives a shit?" I said, as put my foot on the gas pedal and took off. All of a sudden, I had lost my appetite.

By the time I reached home I was exhausted. I hated seeing Wasuan with someone else. All this time I thought his life was at a standstill without me. Maybe, that's because subconsciously I didn't want him to move on. And, Tone—he's a whole 'nother disaster. I didn't even feel like dealing with the likes of his lying ass right now. His card had been pulled, so if he wanted to talk to me, then he was gonna have to make the call, because I sure as hell wasn't going to.

Pregnant? What the hell was I thinking? I wasn't in control of my own situation. It was time for me to get a grip, though, before I ended up getting played worse than my mother had ever been played. The thought of that happening made me feel nauseous. To keep me from throwing up, I shut off my brain, turned off my cell phone and the ringer on my home phone, and took myself to bed.

Hours later, I jumped up out of my sleep, startled by Tone standing over me.

"Oh my God. You scared me, Tone."

"My bad. You just looked so beautiful laying there. I couldn't help but stand here and watch you."

You're so full of it, I thought. Casanova was gonna have to come better than that, because I wasn't buying his bullshit or his charm this time. I looked around my bedroom.

"What time is it?" I asked.

"A little after four."

"In the morning?" I took a deep breath, turned my back towards him, and pulled the covers over my head to go back to sleep. *Four in the fucking morning. I guess his ass had a lot of explaining to do to the Mrs.*

"Enychi? Get up for a minute, please."

"For what, Tone?" I didn't even wanna hear his explanation at this time of morning.

" 'Cause, I know you probably mad at me, right?"

"Why should I be mad at you? It's obvious that I'm just a piece of pussy on the side that you don't give a shit about. So no, I'm not mad at you for being a fucking liar and a dog, but I'm sure your pregnant wife was pretty pissed off about it!"

"Yo, come on, Nych. Get up. Let me explain."

I caught a slight chill from the way Tone said my name, because Nych is what Wasuan used to call me. My mind drifted. *Hum, I wonder if Wasuan is still with that girl?* Running into Wasuan and his little girlfriend earlier bothered me more than finding out about Tone and his wife having another baby. Sometimes I wondered if leaving Wasuan was the right thing to do. Things had gotten bad between us, real bad, but maybe I should've tried to hang in there a little longer, instead of running to Tone. If I just would've hung in there, maybe we would have been alright.

"Okay, go ahead. Explain," I sat up in the bed and examined each one of my freshly painted, French-manicured nails.

"A'ight. First I wanna apologize for that bullshit my wife pulled. She be buggin' the fuck out sometimes."

I looked at him with disgust. "Well, she is your wife! And I expected for me and her to bump heads one day while I was managing your store. But I didn't expect her to be pregnant. That's the part that's confusing me. So explain that part to me. If you and her ain't together 'like that,' then how the hell she get pregnant, Tone? And why didn't you tell me?"

"Honestly, my only explanation for not telling you is because I ain't wanna lose you, and me getting her pregnant again was just something that just happened. A mistake, that's it."

"How many months is she, anyway?"

"She around five or six months. But you gotta believe me when I tell you it ain't like that between me and her."

"That's what you say, but I sure as hell can't tell. And five months wasn't that long ago." He had gotten her pregnant three months before we hooked up, but my problem is, shouldn't he have told me?

"You're right, it wasn't long ago. I slipped up, but me and Natalie ain't been on good terms for over a year now. We just don't click like that no more. So, her wanting to have another baby . . . I can't even tell you what that's about."

"Well, don't you think that you and her not clicking might have something to do with you creeping around on her? Because she made it pretty clear to me that I'm not the first."

"Come on, of course she gon' say that. She tryna get you out the picture," Tone said, while the nervous grin on his face insinuated that he was lying through his teeth.

"Well, should I blame her?"

"Yo, whose side are you on?"

"Tone, it's not about sides, it's about right and wrong."

"Yo, listen to me, 'cause I see where this is going. Natalie is my wife, ain't no denying that. She's a beautiful woman, a good mother to my kids, and she takes care of whatever I need her to.

But the chemistry between us—that shit's dead. The only reason I'm still with her, beside my kids and the years she put in, is because most of the shit I own is in her name—the store, our crib, and all of my cars; and I ain't ready to lose all that. She knows she could fuck me in a lot of ways if she wanted to. And I know she could've been took all my shit and bounced on me a long time ago, but she hasn't. So, in return I try to be the best husband and father I can be, by loving my kids and making sure Natalie and my little girls are straight.

"But you—I really care about you for real. I see good things happening for us."

"Oh, yeah?" I laughed. "Well, did you see good things happening between you and all the other women you had working in the store before me?"

"Come on yo, it wasn't even like that. Them bitches ain't mean shit to me."

"And I do?" I rolled my eyes and pouted. "Why? You trusted them bitches to manage your store, and I'm sure you was dropping dough on them the same way you drop it on me. So please tell me what you've done differently, that makes me stand out from the rest?"

"Man, listen! Outside of my wife, can't none of them bitches say I gave them a place to stay, bought 'em a car or a fuckin' storefront. Shit, I'm tryna make sure you straight, whether you stay with me or not—and I ain't even been fuckin' you for a full three months yet. So, damn, if that ain't enough for you to see how the fuck I feel about you, then I don't know what else I could do. And, yo, since that day I seen you pull up on the block to see that nigga, Wasuan, I thought to myself, *What the fuck is she doing with him?* So, hell yeah, I saw an opportunity and took it. It was never about no money. I put pressure on that nigga 'cause I wanted you. And that ain't no bullshit."

"Okay, so if it wasn't about the money, then don't take the rest of it from him," I told him.

"What?" Tone frowned. "You still care about that dude, don't you?"

"No, I don't," I lied. "I'm just tired of feeling like our relationship is based on a debt, that's all. It's stupid and it's time for you to dead it. You got me now!"

"And that's what's up!" Tone smiled. "Besides, I ain't stressing that li'l forty grand the nigga owe me. If I was hard up for it, I would've been brought heat to his punk ass. I can't front though, I do like making that nigga sweat," he admitted.

"Okay, but that's over with now, right?"

"Yeah, I guess. As long as you ain't tryna get back with that nigga, it's deaded."

"Good." I was glad I could at least do that for Wasuan.

"A'ight, but you know you stuck with me, right?" Tone said with a grim look on his face.

That's what you think, I thought to myself. "I can live with that. You just better make it your business to show up to my graduation next Saturday," I told him.

The seriousness in his voice changed. "Come on now," he smiled. "I wouldn't miss that for nothing in the world."

"Good! Now come to bed," I said, moving over from his side of the bed to mine.

WASUAN

Running into Enychi the other day triggered some feelings that I was trying hard to rid myself off. And, of all days, I had to bump into her while I was out with Latavia. That shit must've sparked up some kind of feelings for Enychi, too, cause ol' girl went off. She caught me by surprise with that one. It's obvious, if a nigga tricking off on her like that, he gotta be feeling her. Shit, I wore them shoes, so I knew Enychi had that ability to make a nigga go for broke. Funny thing was, I also knew Enychi well enough to know that all that material shit might've been all good, but homegirl was frontin'. She wasn't happy with that nigga Tone. I could feel it.

As I stared at the TV screen and then over at Latavia sleeping next to me, I felt trapped my damn self. I checked the time on the cable box. It was just a quarter to eleven. Still early, and here I am lying up in bed with this chick, like we was some old-ass married couple. I had to get up outta there to get some air for real, because shorty was smothering me. I got up, and while I was getting dressed a video from Usher came on BET. I'd never seen it before, but not only did the flame effects in his video grab my attention, the words in this song, "Let it Burn," had me stuck. I sat on the edge of the bed and watched the whole video.

Damn, I felt that nigga's pain, but fuck it! Let it burn, right? With that lasting thought, I threw on my timbs and hit the streets.

One my way to the block I called Mel to find out where that nigga was at.

"Aye, what up, my nigga? You still playing house, or what?" Mel said when he answered.

"Man, shorty won't let a nigga breathe, word up. I just broke out and left her ass at the crib, sleeping."

"So, what's up? What you tryna get into?"

"Nothing crazy, I was gon' hit the block for a minute and see what's going on, that's all."

"A'ight, yo, let me drop my shorty off and I'll meet you over there in, like, twenty minutes, a'ight?"

"No doubt that'll work. I'll see you then."

"A'ight, out!" Mel said as he hung up.

Mel pulled up on the block about fifteen minutes after me. I was standing out there talking to my nigga Durty and a few other cats that was on the corner.

"What up, fellas?" Mel said as he hopped out his whip and greeted everybody with a pound.

"Oh, we chillin', nigga," Durty answered.

"I see that. But what y'all niggas wanna get into?"

"My dough is a'ight right now, so I'm wit whatever." Durty patted the bulge in the pocket of his Akademiks jeans.

"What up with you, Wa-boogie? You on a short leash tonight, or you tryna hang out?" Mel was tryna call a nigga out, I see.

"Come on, dawg," I said. "I ain't on nobody's leash. So I'm with whatever."

"A'ight, that's what's up. Let's roll to Sue's Rendezvous, then."

"Nigga, let me find out you hooked on that stripper shit hard like that."

"Yo Wa, man, them chicks that be up in Sue's, they a'ight!" Mel looked like he was about to drool at the mouth just from thinking about 'em.

"Yeah, I hear you, nigga."

Mel wasn't lying, the girls up in Sue's looked like something straight out of *King* magazine. It was Celebrity Tuesday, so the spot was packed with everything from NBA ballplayers to them straight-hustlin' dudes with long money and that 'hood celebrity status. Anybody that was somebody was at a table popping bottles, with a crowd of chicks around them.

We bought our bottles, sat down at a table, checked out the scenery, and tossed a few dollars at every chick that hit the stage. We got our drink on, and laughs, too, as the Tuesday-night host, Ed Lover, cracked jokes and talked shit over the mike about some of the dancers.

Shit was running smooth. I know I was having a good time—that is, until the nigga Tone walked in with some big-tittie bitch on his arm and a small entourage of niggas trailing two feet behind him. They all came and stood not far from our table. My high was blown. I couldn't stand the sight of that dude.

"Yo, what up Mel? What up Durty?" Tone yelled over the loud music.

Mel nodded. "What's up?" and Durty answered, "We chillin'."

"Yo, Wa, you cool?" Mel must've known that Tone's presence had me tight.

I wasn't gonna let it fuck up my night, though. "I'm good," I told him.

"Good! Fuck that nigga, a'ight? I'm about go and get this lap dance. I'll be back," Mel looked me in the eyes. "You gon' be a'ight though?" he asked, as he got up from the table to go to the back room where the private dances were performed.

"Yo, man, I ain't thinking about that dude! Do you, my man, I'ma go take this leak, though." I got up from the table, too. "Yo, Durty, hold it down," I said, referring to our table. "I'll be right back."

"Oh, no doubt! You know I got this," Durty responded, tipping the bottle of Grey Goose to his mouth, then chasing it with a bottle of cranberry juice.

As I was shaking my joint off to put it back in my pants, Tone walked in the bathroom.

"Well, well, well, look who we have here!" Tone laughed. "Yo, where my money at, nigga! I bet ya bitch ass miss Enychi's fine ass now, don't you? She a piece of work, too. Whoo!" He acted as though he caught a chill, then said, "That girl will fuck me all day if I let her."

By now, I was sure this nigga Tone knew he wasn't getting another dime from me, and if he was gonna do something, he had plenty of opportunities to make his move. So on the real, I was starting to feel like this nigga was all bark and no bite. And he'd been getting his rocks off at my expense long enough.

. . .

"Yo, Tone, fuck you! What? You a fucking homo or sumpthin'? You stay tryna ride my dick, nigga! If you gon' do something, bring it, yo!" I stepped to him. "I right here, nigga. What!" Enough was enough, my life could've ended right then and there, but I ain't give a fuck, I was sick of Tone's shit.

"Nigga, back the fuck up!" he said. "You talking real tough right now, come talk that shit outside."

Tone was a big dude compared to me. He had to be about six-five and at least 270 pounds, but it didn't seemed like he was all that tough when he wasn't strapped.

"Nigga, fuck outside! I'm here. What? You ain't got ya gun with you now?" I knew he wasn't packing nothing, because them security dudes at the door wasn't letting no niggas slide through them doors with shit. Before Tone could say anything, or make a move, two big bouncer dudes walked up in there.

"Yo, if there a problem fellas, y'all gon' have to take it someplace else," said the security dude. He was wearing corn-rows and looked just like a darker version of Forest Whitaker.

"No, doubt," Tone said, cutting his eyes at me as he walked out the bathroom.

Forest looked at me and said, "Y'all cool?"

When I got back to the table, Durty was up in the waitress's face trying to holla at her, Mel wasn't back from his lap dance yet, and Tone and his crew was now seated at a table off to the far left from where I was sitting. I kept my eye on that nigga, though, just to make sure he ain't parking first. Just then, Mel came back to the table.

"I'm ready to go," I told him. I didn't want to be the one to break up the party, but I wasn't feeling this no more.

"Yo, don't tell me you gon' let dude run you up outta here," Mel said.

"Nah, it ain't that! I'm just ready to go, dawg, that's all." I didn't even bother to tell Mel what happened.

"A'ight, nigga, whatever," Mel said. I didn't care about that nigga's attitude, but I was mad at myself for not driving my own car. "Yo, dawg, come on, we out." Mel tapped Durty on his shoulder, aggravated.

ENYCHI

Bumping into Tone's wife, Natalie, at the store was only the beginning. The bitch was a straight psychopath, and she made it her business to make sure I knew that. A couple of nights after the store incident, Tone and I were out grabbing a bite to eat all the way out in City Island, at Sammy's, when out of nowhere Natalie walked over to our table wearing a BCBG sweat suit, with her hair pulled back in a ponytail, like she was looking for a fight.

"Tone! You a lying muthafucka! What the fuck are you doing here with this bitch?" she yelled.

Tone looked up from the menu in a state of shock. "Yo, come on, Nat! What the fuck you do, follow me?" Tone said, as he jumped up from the booth and stood in front of her.

"You damn right, muthafucka! I'm tired of you fuckin' around with all these different bitches. And bitch, you ain't shit, running around with my fuckin' husband. Wait 'til I have my muthafuckin' son, you trifling-ass, home-wrecking bitch. I'm beat the shit out of you, ho!" Natalie said, directing her anger towards me as she started to cause a huge scene.

"Yo, Nat, chill the fuck out, you be playing your mutha-fuckin' self. You followed me all the way the fuck out here to make a fool of yourself, man. Yo, just go home, please!" Tone said.

"Tone, I'm not going nowhere without you. I'm tired of you doing this shit to me," Natalie said as she started to cry. "You said you wasn't fuckin' with that bitch. I been with you for fifteen years; I take care of your fuckin' kids, I do everything for you, and this is how the fuck you gon' play me. I'm tired of your shit, Tone! So, either you gon' leave with me now, or I'ma go home and set fire to all your shit, and you ain't gon' never see you kids again. That's my word on our unborn son!"

I was so embarrassed. People were staring at us, while I sat quietly in the midst of Natalie's meltdown. I had to admit, I felt sorry for her.

"Yo, come on, man! Let me walk you to your car." Tone grabbed Natalie by her arm and turned to me and said, "I'll be right back."

"No, the fuck he won't." Natalie rolled her eyes at me so hard I thought she was gonna lose them.

Minutes later, Tone returned to our table. I wasn't happy about what had just gone down, but I was glad to see that Tone had his situation under control. "Yo, this chick is bugging the fuck out," he said. "So, just take my car, a'ight. Let me take her home, 'for I end up going to jail tonight." He handed me some money and his car keys.

Oh, so he just gon' leave me, here? I gave him a dirty look. "Yeah, alright, whatever Tone!" I said, snatching his keys and the money from his hand.

He walked back out, and I left, so disgusted I didn't know

what to do. As soon as I got in the car I pulled my cell phone from my purse and dialed Denita.

"What's up girl?" she answered.

"'Nita, you dressed?"

"No, but I could throw something on. Why, what's up?"

"Girl, I'ma need you to do that, 'cause I'm coming to get you. I need a fucking drink, right now."

"Why, what happened?"

"Girl, me and Tone went to Sammy's to get something to eat, and guess who shows up? His wife, Natalie!"

"Get the fuck outta here! How she knew ya'll was all the way out there?"

"She followed us, that's how."

"From where? Ya crib?" Denita inquired.

"Oh shit, she had to! That bitch must know where the fuck I stay at now, 'cause Tone came over and got me."

"Well, what she say?"

"Girl, Natalie went off. She said when she have her baby she gon' beat the shit out of me," I laughed as I thought about it.

"What? She said that? Girl, why wait 'til she have that baby? Shit, I would've jumped on her ass right then and there."

"I ain't going to jail for fighting her pregnant ass."

"Well, I don't give a fuck! I'd fight her pregnant ass. That bitch bad enough to talk shit and make threats while she pregnant, then she bad enough to get her ass kicked while she pregnant."

"Nah, not while she's pregnant. The baby ain't got shit to do with her silly ass."

"Her pregnant ass shouldn't be out getting silly then! Nychi, I'm tellin' you, girl, you too nice."

173

"Anyway, girl, Tone gave me his car keys and left with his wife."

"Oh, hell no! Fuck that nigga! Yeah, hurry up and come get me. Let's go get a couple drinks and then drive that nigga's shit over to South Road, down by the tracks, and torch it, girl."

I bust out laughing. " 'Nita you crazy."

"Laugh if you want to. I'm dead serious. That nigga wrong for that."

"Well, if we blow up his car, how the fuck we gon' get home?"

"We'll take a fucking cab, that's how!"

"Nah, I ain't gon' do no shit like that. Besides, we'd trip, too, if one of us was married and our man was fucking around on us, so I can't even be mad at her."

"Enychi, you always gotta be the voice of reason. Fuck that bitch! Her man cheating on her is her fucking problem, because trust and believe me when I tell you this, if Tone wasn't fucking you, he'd be fucking somebody else. Shit, it's her fault she can't keep her man from sticking his dick elsewhere, so fuck her. Where you at anyway? You got me all hype and shit. My ass need a drink now, too."

"I'm five minutes away, so hurry up and finish getting dressed. I'll see you in a minute."

"A'ight, bet."

Just as I was pulling up, Denita was already walking out of her building. "Hey, girl," I said, as she hopped in the car.

"What's up, where we going?"

"I don't know. Did you eat yet?" I asked.

"Earlier, but we can go get a bite to eat, 'cause I know you gotta be hungry, since Tone got your mouth all ready for some seafood and let his bitch ruin y'all dinner plans."

"Girl, don't remind me. I was ready to sink my teeth into one of them broiled lobster tails, too!" We both laughed.

"It's only nine o'clock. You wanna go to Red Lobster?" Denita suggested.

"Yeah, that'll work."

Just as I pulled up in the resturant's parking lot, Tone was ringing my cell phone.

"Girl, that's his sorry ass calling me now," I said to Denita.

"Fuck him, don't even answer it. I bet he done took that bitch home, filled her head with all kinds of lies about you and him, and now he ready to fill your head with some bullshit too."

For a moment I thought about answering, but instead I pressed the ignore button hoping that'll set his ass straight. "Uh-huh, and I am so tired of him and his drama, girl. Come on, let's go eat!"

After we ate, Denita and I remained in Red Lobster, getting twisted off frozen margaritas and strawberry daiquiris, until the manager threw us the hell out because it was closing time. We was so drunk, Denita ended up having to spend the night with me, because I only had one stop in me: There was no way I could take her home and then drive myself home.

The following morning, Denita and I both jumped up out of our sleep, startled by the annoying sound of someone ringing the downstairs buzzer to my apartment. Denita looked down at the watch on her wrist. "Damn girl, who the fuck is that ringing your bell like that at eight o'clock in the damn morning?" She definitely wasn't a morning person, especially not after having too much drink the night before.

"I don't know. It's probably Tone. You know I didn't answer his call last night, so he's probably wondering what's up."

I got up out of bed and walked into my living room and over to the intercom box on the wall near the front door. "Yeah, who is it?" I said, with grogginess in my tone.

"It's me, Natalie! I need to talk to you, right now, bitch!"

I stepped back from the intercom, appalled. *No she* didn't *come to my house.* I tiptoed back to my bedroom. "Denita, that bitch is downstairs right now!" I whispered.

"Natalie? You can't be serious!"

"Yes, girl."

"Oh, see now, she asking for a beatdown."

Natalie started ringing my buzzer recklessly, and this time Denita went to the intercom.

"Bitch, you gotta be crazy! Why the fuck is you ringing my bell like that?" she said, posing as me.

"'Cause I wanna talk to you about my husband, ho! So bring your ass downstairs!" Natalie yelled.

"No, what you need to do is go talk to your husband and leave me the fuck alone. 'Cause if I come downstairs, I'm beating your pregnant ass, bitch!"

"What! Ho, if you don't come down, I'm bring my pregnant ass to your door, bitch! Let me in this muthafucka!" Natalie started kicking and banging on the downstairs door.

While Denita was getting her kicks outta amping up Natalie, I ran over to the phone and called Tone.

"Why you ain't answer my call last night?" Tone asked, as soon as he answered his cell.

"Look, forget all that. You need to get over here and get your wife before she beat down the downstairs door. Because I've been real calm with her ass, but she can't be showing up where I rest at!"

"What?"

"You heard me! Natalie's downstairs ringing the hell outta my buzzer and tryna break the damn door down. She's fucking insane, Tone!"

"Damn, yo! I don't know why the fuck you had to tell her I got you that shop. She done lost her muthafuckin' mind over that shit."

"Well, I didn't tell her on purpose! She was getting real slick with the mouth, and it slipped out. Anyway, she knows now. So, all I'm saying is, you need to get over here right now and handle her!"

"Yeah, a'ight, just don't open the door."

"I'm not, just hurry up!" Now all I had to do was keep Denita from breaking out the Vaseline and going downstairs to whip Natalie's ass.

Fifteen minutes after I hung up the phone with Tone, the ruckus stopped; and after an hour of talking about Natalie's crazed and deranged self, Denita and I fell back to sleep.

I assumed Tone was trying to lay low, since things had gotten out of control with him and his wife, but I wasn't gonna be waiting in the wings until he secured his position with her again.

I dialed his number, expecting his voice mail, when, surprisingly, he answered. "What up, ma? I was just thinking about you."

"Is that right?" I said.

"Yeah, why you sounding like that?"

"Why you think?"

"Come on, you know what I've been going through. That chick is off her rocker right now, and I don't want her harassing you."

"Yeah, well that's why I'm calling you. I don't think we should see each other anymore."

"Yo, that's nonsense right there. You mines," Tone said, as if he owned me.

"Tone, it's not working out. Besides, we both knew this wasn't a long-term thing."

"Well, I'm ready to make it long-term. That's what I'm

working on right now. I'm getting all my important shit up out of the crib on the low. The house, furniture, and all that other shit don't mean nothing to me, she could keep all that. I ain't even taking my clothes. I'll buy some more. That's how bad I wanna get the fuck away from Nat and all her craziness. But in the meantime, we gon' have to meet up in hotels until you find us another crib."

"What? Wait a minute? I don't wanna find another crib," I said with attitude.

"Come on, yo, we gon' have to."

I put my hand on my forehead. "Tone, this is moving a little too fast for me."

"A'ight, check this out. After your graduation, I'ma take you somewhere nice, so we can chill and talk about everything that we need to work out, a'ight?"

"Tone—"

"Look, I gotta go. I love you."

Tone shocked me with those three words. He'd never said that to me before. The idea of being in love again gave me butterflies, but as fast as it came, it passed. Whether or not Tone meant what he said, I didn't love him back, and it was over no matter how much he wanted to pretend that it wasn't.

After I got off the phone, I decided to finish up the final alteration on my graduation dress. "Oh shit!" I yelled as I looked over at the clock radio and hopped up from my bed. It was almost two. I had a hair appointment scheduled for 2:15 and hadn't even showered yet. I didn't have time to now, so I just threw on yesterday's clothes and rushed out of my apartment.

Two hours later, I walked up out of the salon feeling like a real diva, with my silky straight wrap. I was so ready and excited about graduaing tomorrow that there was nothing that could steal my joy. Or so I thought.

I almost choked when I approached my Benz and saw the white spray paint and deep scratches that were carved into the silver paint. I ran towards my car and screamed, "Ooh, I can't stand that bitch!"

I started to cry as I stared at the words "bitch, homewrecka, and ho," keyed into the hood and passenger door of my ride. There wasn't a doubt in my mind about who did this. It had Natalie's name written all over it. Immediately, I grabbed my cell phone from my purse and dialed Tone. I was so pissed I almost snapped my phone in half when his voice mail came on.

"Ahh, I hate his ass, too!" I yelled as I slammed down the hood of my cell. I opened my car door, got in, and waited a few seconds before I dialed Tone again. "Tone, this is Enychi. Call me back *as soon* as you get this message!" I didn't want to tell him his wife fucked up my car on his voice mail, because he might take his time to call me back.

I sat in my parked car for a few moments to think.

I can't drive to my graduation with this shit keyed all over my car. Tone hasn't call me back yet, and Lord only knows, I don't feel like hearing Denita's mouth about this. Not now, anyway.

I know! I'll take it back to Paulie, the guy at the dealership!

I started my car and headed over to the Benz dealership where Tone bought the car from.

As soon as I got out the car and walked into the showroom, I spotted Paulie shaking hands with what looked like another happy customer.

"Aye, how are you, beautiful?" Paulie said in that strong Italian accent of his. As he made his way towards me, he must've noticed the surprised look on my face, because he went on to say, "I never forget the face of a good customer or the company he keeps. How is my friend, anyway? I haven't seen him in awhile."

Assuming he was talking about Tone, I answered, "Oh, he's doing fine." I gave him a fake smile. "He just been a little busy, that's all."

"Oh, I'm sure. So, what can I do for you today, beautiful? Are you still enjoying the car, or what?" Paulie asked.

"Yes, I love it! Actually that's why I'm here. I was hoping that you could fix it for me," I signaled for him to follow me outside and take a look at it.

"Whoa!" Paulie shook his head. "The Mrs., huh?" he asked.

I was too embarrassed to verbally answer that question, so I just shook my head yes.

"Yeah, it's a bummer, but it happens to the best of us. You guys been dating long?"

"Can you fix the car?" I wasn't comfortable, nor did I feel it was appropriate for him to be all up in my business like that.

"Sure, we can fix it. It's gonna run you, let's say somewhere around, ahh, a ballpark figure of three thousand."

"That's fine. Now, can you fix it today?"

"No, we're gonna have to paint it, and that's gonna take a couple of days, maybe even a week."

"Oh, no! I can't wait a week. You see, I need my car back by tomorrow." I was in tears all over again.

"Look, I'll tell you what I can do. Since your friend is a very good friend and customer of mine, I can give you a loaner car. Now, it's not fully loaded like yours, but it's the same make. Is that okay, beautiful?"

"Yes, that'll be great!" I said. Paulie gave me the keys to a very similar Benz, the only difference to me was the leather seats were black, and mines were beige, and that worked for me. I felt a lot better, knowing that my car could be fixed and that I wouldn't have to drive around with slander written all over it. But this mess with Natalie had to stop right now. Tone hadn't even called me back yet, and I didn't bother to call him again, either. Tomorrow was my graduation, and all I wanted to do now was go home, take a hot bath, and get a good night's rest. I'd deal with Tone's ass after the ceremony.

E N Y C H I

"Enychi M. Carter." The crowded auditorium soared with rounds of applause and the loud sounds of cheers while I stood to my feet, hearing my name called. Stepping out into the aisle in my burgundy-and-yellow cap and gown, I welcomed the feeling of achievement as I made my way to the podium, This day had finally arrived. *Yes! I did it. I'm here!* I thought.

I had looked forward to this day my entire life, and it felt just as good as I'd imagined it would. As I received my degree, I saw my moms standing in the audience with tears in her eyes and a proud look on her face.

After the ceremony, I rushed over to Denita. "Come on. I want you to meet my moms," I said, as I grabbed her by her hand. Together, we went looking for Tone, so I could introduce him to my mother and her husband.

I searched around but couldn't find Tone anywhere. A strong feeling of disappointment came over me. I know I told him I didn't want to be with him anymore, but he knew how important his support meant to me.

"No, the fuck he didn't. Denita, I know Tone couldn't have missed the most important day of my life."

"Nah, he's a lot of things, but I don't think he's that stupid. He gotta be in here somewhere." Denita said.

Maybe something happened to him. Check your phone to see if he left a message, I told myself. A tragedy of some sort was the only excuse I'd accept for his absence.

"Damn, I left my cell phone in the car."

"Oh, Enychi, I am so proud of you, darling," my mom said, as she came hurrying towards me and Denita with open arms. My mother was Cherokee Indian mixed with Black, so she had very fine jet black hair that hung past her shoulders. She has a medium-brown complexion and is not fat, but on the thick side. She is a very pretty thirty-eight-year-old, who didn't look like she aged much since the last time I saw her.

She should *be proud of me, because me making it was no thanks to her,* I thought, as we hugged. Her husband, Pastor Burns, wrapped his arms around me, too, and offered his congratulations.

"Thanks. Ma, I want you guys to meet my best friend here, Denita."

"Hello, Mrs. Burns and Pastor Burns. It's nice to finally meet you guys. I've heard so much about you."

"Yes, congrats to you, too, young lady," Pastor Burns said.

"Enychi, you cool? 'Cause I'm gonna run over to my peoples now, a'ight?" Denita said.

"Oh, okay, yeah. I'm good, girl." I gave her a hug and said, "I'll call you later, all right?"

I didn't want my mother to sense that there was a problem, and to start meddling in my business.

"Well, come on, darling. Let's go celebrate." I took off my graduation robe to show off my own personal design, once she said that.

My moms threw her arms around me. "Oh, honey, that dress is beautiful! You look fabulous, sweetie," she said, as we made our way toward the exit. I was glad that she had a good eye for style.

"Honey, are you gonna ride with us?" My moms asked.

"No, Mother. But you guys can follow me. I know this nice little Italian restaurant that's not too far from here. Is that okay?"

"Sure, that sounds great," she said, as she glanced at her husband for his approval.

As I hit the button on the key to deactivate the alarm on my loaner SLSS, my mom's eyes lit up like Christmastime.

"Wow! Whose Benz is that, Enychi?" she asked.

"Mine." I lied, but it was just like the one I have, so what the hell?

"Yours? How could you afford a note like that?"

"Come on, Ma. Can we please go eat now?"

"Okay, but I still want to know how you're affording a car like that, Enychi."

I ignored her and got in the car. I couldn't believe my mother. She had the nerve to put me on the spot like that. I swear, I wanted to say something slick, but I'd never disrespect my mother to her face.

The first thing I did when I sat in the loaner was check my phone to see if I had any messages. I did: one—from a blocked number. Automatically assuming it was Tone, I called my voice mail, but, to my surprise, the message was from Wasuan.

"Enychi," he said, "by the time you get this message you'll be an official college graduate, and that's what's up. Wish I could've been there. I know this message might not mean much to you now, but I just wanted to congratulate you and say that I'm proud of you. I still love and always think about you. Take care."

My heart felt like it had stopped beating, as the tears started to run down my face. Deep down, I missed him so much; and the fact that he remembered this day said a lot. At that point I'd made up my mind. As far as I was concerned, it was over between me and Tone.

As soon as we arrived at the restaurant, my mother's husband excused himself and went to the rest room.

"Young lady, where did you get the money to afford a car like that?" my mother whispered. "Was it that drug-dealing boyfriend of yours? I hope he doesn't have you mixed up in his illegal mess. Please, tell me you're not into anything illegal, Enychi Michelle Carter! In the name of Jesus, you better answer me, child!"

"No, I didn't get the money from doing anything illegal. Okay? You happy now?"

I could tell from the frown on her face that my response didn't sit well with her. She wanted details and I wasn't gonna give her any. "And why should it matter anyway?" I added. "It ain't like you were sending me any money to help me pay for school, or a place to stay, or even to make ends meet. You just up and left and started yourself a new life, didn't you? So don't come back now, after four years, and wanna question my survival skills. After all, I am your daughter, and we both know: Mama did what she had to do to get by, right Mother?"

I couldn't help myself. I had to take it there because she was so concerned about how I got the car; but, for four years, never once did she wonder how I was managing to take care of myself and get through school.

My mother gasped. She had an appalled look on her face, but that didn't stop me, because I was just getting started. "And, yes, Mother, I got myself a nice apartment, that car, and my own boutique, too. So you see, you taught me well. I managed to make it in this world, just like you did."

Just as I finished my sentence her husband came back to the table, and for the rest of our meal my mother and I ate in silence.

Later that evening, I felt bad about what I said—but not enough to apologize, because she needed to hear how I felt. Even if I had taken my frustrations about the whole missing Wasuan and hating Tone bit out on her, it was way overdue. And, as happy as I was to see my mother make it to my graduation; I was even happier to see her go back home that same night.

Instead of sticking with my plan to hang out with Denita, so we could have a little fun and celebrate, I went home. She was mad at me, but I knew she'd get over it. Besides, I was too beat to enjoy myself. I got in my bed at ten o'clock, but I tossed and turned until around 11:30.

I was completely restless, and I couldn't stop thinking about the message Wasuan had left. Eventually, I gave in to my pride, reached over on the night table for my cell, and dialed Wasuan's house number.

"Hello," the voice of that ghetto girl came over the line and I hung up. *Must be serious. She's answering his phone now.* I knew I shouldn't have called him. I slammed myself back down in the bed and snatched the covers over my head.

. . .

What time is it? I wondered, as I woke up to the sound of my cell phone ringing. Almost missing the call as I searched through my crumpled bedspread for my phone, I saw when I found it that it was Tone.

"What?" I answered with an attitude.

"Hey, ma, I know it's kinda early, but, shit, I was up all night." Tone sounded like there was something wrong, but I brushed it off.

Checking my wristwatch, I saw that it was six in the morning. "What do you want, Tone?" I took a deep breath. "You couldn't call me yesterday to say you wouldn't be at my graduation, so why are you calling me now?" I said, as I rolled my eyes and pursed my lips, awaiting his bullshit reponse.

"I know; but, yo, I had every intention of being at your graduation. Believe that, but my wife was in a car accident and we lost the baby. A little *boy* at that!"

"Oh! My God, Tone. I'm so sorry to hear that." I could hear the devastation in his voice. He loved his kids, and he talked about those little girls of his all the time. Tone had joked a few times about how he wanted a son; and even though the doctors had already confirmed that it was a boy, he wanted to wait and see for himself. He believed God gave him three girls as payback for all the nasty and freaky things he'd done to other fathers, who had tried to protect their precious daughters. So I knew he had to be grieving hard over the loss of his son.

"I don't know. Maybe this shit is my fault, you know? Stressing her out like that." There was a moment of silence. "Anyway," he continued, "I'm about to take Nat home. We been in this fucking hospital for at least eighteen hours, so I'm tired as hell right now, but I'ma try and see you later on tonight, a'ight?"

"No, that's alright. You should be with your wife and kids tonight, Tone."

"You think so?"

"Of course I do."

"A'ight. Well, I'ma see you tomorrow then."

"Uh-uh, Tone. That's not such a good idea, either." I was tired of Tone and Natalie, but the fact that she had just lost their baby, and he was on the phone trying to see me, just confirmed my decision yet again, because, I might've hated Natalie for what she did to my car, but I wouldn't wish her situation on anyone, and I damn sure didn't want a man like Tone. "It's over, Tone," I said. "I don't wanna be caught up in the middle of your shit anymore."

"What? What the fuck you mean?" Tone's voice got louder. "So, what? You flipping on me now, 'cause I couldn't come to that fucking graduation?"

"Tone, there's a whole lot of reasons for me to flip on you, and you know it. I won't put up with your situation anymore. That's all. You got a wife and kids. Be with them."

"Yo, you a fucked-up individual, you know that? I just told you I lost my fucking son, and now you wanna hit me with the *you ain't putting up with my situation* bullshit? Bitch, I *own* you! And unless you gonna give me all that shit back I bought for you, *and* got forty Gs for me, that's how its gon' be. Now, like I said a minute ago, I'ma chill with the wife tonight and see you tomorrow!"

Tone had finally exposed his true colors, and why wasn't I surprised? After he hung up, I sat up in my bed, feeling a little intimidated by the way he came at me.

Fortunately, for the next couple of days, Tone never showed up. Still, I moved around with caution, because he and his wife were crazy, if you asked me. I started putting my time into what was important to me, and that was my boutique's grand opening.

Me and Denita got most of the top distributors to do business with us, so things were about to take off. All we needed was a name. After one day of heavy brainstorming, we finally came up with one: The Red Carpet Boutique. We were both so excited.

Outside of being happy about the progress we had made, the thought of Tone taking my store from me kept entering my head. Although I knew, with it being in my name, he wouldn't stand much of a chance, I didn't know the lines he'd cross to get it back. I told Denita about that last conversation with Tone, and she decided to stay with me at my place for awhile.

"Don't worry, girl," Denita said. "I got your back, and what I can't cover, this twenty-two that my brother gave me will." She pulled a small gun from her Gucci bag.

"Put that thing away!" I yelled

"Enychi, stop being so scary, girl. You need to learn how to use one of these." Denita pointed the gun at the wall and pretended to shoot. "Shit, you're about to open the boutique soon, and you gon' need some kind of protection up in there, 'cause I can't be there with you all the time," she said.

"I'll get a security guard. Now put that shit away!" I demanded.

"A'ight, calm down." Denita rolled her eyes as she tucked the gun back down in her purse. "In the meantime, I'ma let my brother know what's up, and that I'll be staying with you, just in case that nigga Tone starts to feel froggish and wanna leap."

"Denita, you know Mel's gonna run back and tell Wasuan that I got a beef with Tone, and I really don't wanna have them all up in my business like that." As soon as I said that, my cell phone started to ring. "Oh shit, 'Nita, that's Tone calling me right now." I got so nervous, I started to fidget. "What should I do?"

"Just answer it so he don't think you're ducking him."

"But I am!" I responded confused.

"I know that, but his ass don't need to know that. Just answer!"

"Hey, baby," I answered.

"What took you so long to answer?" Tone asked.

"Um, I'm in the car and my music was up kinda loud."

"Oh, a'ight! So, what's good? I gave you a couple of days to get your head right, so we cool again, I hope."

"Yeah, we good," I mumbled.

"Yeah, I kinda figured that." He chuckled. "Anyway, I'ma go see some of my dudes, since I ain't been on the scene in a minute, and after I'm done with that, I'ma get up with you, a'ight?"

"Okay."

"A'ight, then. Later."

I hung up my cell phone. "Now what, Denita?" I said. "He wants to meet up with me later."

"Fuck him! When he calls back, just come up with some type of excuse, that's all."

"Denita, come on, you think he ain't gon' catch on to that?"

"Yeah, he probably will; but until we can come up with something better, just keep hittin' 'em excuses, okay?"

"Alright, I'll try."

W A S U A N

Just as I was starting to get used to Latavia being around all the time, I found out the bitch was stealing from me. I thought I was bugging this morning, when I went in my sock drawer and recounted some money I had for Mel and it was two hundred dollars short. After counting that shit three times, to make sure it was straight before I put it in there, I knew I wasn't tripping. So, with just me and Latavia living up in here, I ain't have to be no rocket scientist to know her ass was the culprit. I wasn't feeling that shit at all, and while she was in the bathroom showering I was tossing all her shit right outside my apartment door. *Fuck that!* I knocked hard on the bathroom door once I was finished with her things.

"What's wrong, boo?" Latavia said, as she opened the door with a towel wrapped around her wet body.

"Come on, let's go!" I snatched her by the arm and started pulling her.

"Wait, where we going?" Latavia grabbed onto the arm of the chair in the living room when she realized I was dragging her ass out the front door. "Stop! What did I do? I ain't got no fuckin' clothes on!" she screamed.

"I don't give a fuck! You should've thought about that shit before you stole from me."

"What?" Latavia looked surprised. "Wait, I was gon' give that back, that's my word, yo! Please, Wa, I'm sorry!" She started to cry. "I still got the money. You can have it back. Please just don't make me leave like this."

"Yo, why you had to steal from me, 'Tav? I mean, if you needed something, you should've just asked me. I would've gave it to you." I was trying to be stern about the shit, but I let her tears get to me. "Go get your shit out the hallway and come back inside," I told her.

Latavia let go of the chair, stood on her tippy toes, and put her arms around me. "I promise it won't happen again, and I'm real sorry that I went out like that to begin with. You're my boo, and I love you!" she said, as them tears dried up quick.

"Yeah, a'ight, whatever," I said. "Just hurry up and get your stuff out the hall before I change my mind."

The next day, I was on my way to take Latavia to Jamaica Avenue to get her nails done, when I stopped by the projects for a minute to holla at Mel and give him that money I had for him. As soon as I pulled up, Mel's moms was looking out the window. I rolled down my window and looked up at her.

She knew exactly what I was about to ask. "He in the back of the building."

"Come on," I said to Latavia. *It's about time I show her off a little bit*, I thought to myself. Besides, I wanted to let my niggas see that I was over that bullshit with Enychi, and I had already moved on.

I walked around to the back, and there was Mel sitting on the bench, talking on the cell. My boy was dressed like he was ready for war, wearing his Army fatigues getup, a fresh pair of brown Timberlands, and a finished, blue 9 mm strapped to his waist. He wasn't alone. There was a group of niggas standing around, and from the looks of things, they were about to get a dice game started.

I stood there and waited for Mel to get off the phone, while I watched as the small crowd of dudes got it popping.

"Yo, what up, Wa?" yelled Durty.

"Aye, what up, Durty? I'm chilling."

"So, what's up? You gon' get up in this game, or what?"

"Nah, I'ma have to pass on that." I looked at him, and then over towards Latavia, who had just sat down on the bench.

"Ahh, man, yo. Why not? These cats don't know what they doing," Durty yelled out again, as he watched the game from the sidelines.

"Yo, come on, Wa. I know you can take these dudes for they loot, man." Speedy cosigned.

"Come on, nigga, come get your roll on," another voice said.

"Go ahead, Wasuan. Why don't you wanna play?" Latavia added.

"'Cause I gotta take you to the ave, that's why!" I said, using that as my excuse.

"Well, I'm not in no rush," she said.

"See, man, your shorty's cool. She ain't in no rush."

As the crowd tried to gas me up to play, I looked at Mel.

He'd just gotten off the phone and shrugged his shoulders like *that's on you.*

"Nah, I'll pass," I said. "I can't fuck with that shit no more, but y'all knock yaselves out."

Mel looked at me and smiled. "That's what's up, baby boy. I proud of you nigga." He stood up and gave me a pound. "Word up, yo, I thought you was about to jump on board."

"I know, I see how you looked at the kid, like you was worried." I handed Mel the money I had for him. "But, yo, that gambling shit, it's a wrap for me. It gotta be, before I end up—"

I couldn't even finish my sentence—after I saw that nigga Tone walking up.

"Aye, yo, I'm out y'all," I said, as I walked over and gave the few dudes that I was cool with a pound.

"A'ight, later my nigga." Durty didn't question my sudden need to get up outta there, because he knew what it was about.

But, of course, Tone wouldn't be Tone if he didn't open his fucking mouth. "Yo, big man, don't leave on account of me." he said.

"Yo, son, you know you got that nigga shook!" said cheatin-ass Chico. I guess he was still bitter about me punching him in his mouth.

"Nah, that nigga wasn't shook when we was up in Sue's that night. He wanted to fight then. Ain't that right, small time?"

"Latavia, let's go," I said, but she didn't budge. She just stood there and looked at me like, *I know you ain't gon' let that nigga dis you like that.*

"I see you done got yaself another one? Yo, how the fuck your pussy-ass be pulling these bad-ass bitches, man? He done got hisself red bone this time." Tone threw back his head and laughed. "Yo, is she up for grabs, too?" he asked.

Mel spoke up. "Yo, man, chill with all that bullshit for real. Dawg, you can't keep hating on my peoples like that, word up. That shit's getting played out, man!"

"Mel, I ain't got no beef with you. But, yo, fuck your peoples. You need to teach his bitch ass how to stand up and be a man, then maybe he'll get some respect."

"Latavia," I handed her my car keys on the sly, "go sit in the car," I said.

"A'ight, boo, handle your business," Latavia whispered, as she took my keys and started walking.

While Tone was still running off at the mouth, I was fuming. I stood there for a minute and I could feel myself turning red as fire. I knew I had let this shit go on for way too long, but it was gon' stop right here and right now.

"Yo, Mel, walk me to my car, I'm outta here," I said, to throw Tone off. But as soon as Mel got up on me, I snatched his nine from his waist, and rushed Tone.

He was so used to sleeping on me that he ain't see me coming. I spazzed out on him, hitting Tone in his head so hard with that nine that I heard his skull crack. But it didn't stop there. I hated that nigga, and the more I rammed the gun in his head the more satisfaction I got. It was like I was possessed and the devil was on my shoulder, laughing and cheering me on, as I beat Tone into a corpse.

Some dudes stood around and watched, while others broke out. I could hear females screaming and children crying, but I didn't care. It was like I was in a trance. Tone's blood splattered all over me, the bench, and the ground. I couldn't stop myself, though. I hit him over and over again—until Mel finally ran up behind me and grabbed me, restraining me. "Come on, man, enough, stop it! Yo, Wasuan, it's over, chill!" he said.

And, suddenly, I snapped out of that state of mind I had been in and realized what I had done. When I saw Tone lying on the ground with his head busted wide open and his blood all over my hand, my stomach felt weak.

He looked like he was dead, and I ain't feel or have one ounce of remorse about it. All I kept saying to myself was *See what the fuck you made me do? Now, who's a bitch-ass now?*

I heard the sounds of police sirens getting closer, and closer, as Mel kept pleading with me, "Yo, Wa, come on, cuz. Snap out of that shit! Run man! Go, get the fuck up outta here. Come on, Wa, please, man." Mel had already taken the bloody gun from me and had it wrapped up in a towel. "Yo, Ma!" he called out, looking up at his mother's window. "Ma!" he repeated, until she came to the window and yelled, "What, Melone! You out here calling me like you done lost your fuckin' min—Oh, my God, Wasuan! What did you do?"

"Yo, Ma, just meet me in the hallway and take this for me, please," Mel said, referring to his bloody gun.

Mel ran into the building's hallway, but I couldn't move. I'm not even sure I wanted to. Tears began to run down my face when I thought about the one place that I tried to avoid going back to—jail!

Still stuck, standing over Tone's limp body, I just stared at him. That's where I stayed until the cops came. I wanted to run then, but where would I run to if I did?

"Put your hands up and get down on the fucking ground! Do

it now!" The policeman ordered, as one cop car after another pulled up and the po-pos surrounded me with their guns drawn.

As I put my hands up over my head and dropped to my knees, I heard Mel's mother yell from the window, "Ya'll mutha-fuckas better not hurt him, neither!"

"Yo, Wa, man, don't worry. I'ma get you a lawyer! Aye, yo, officers, that shit was self-defense," I heard Mel call out as 5-0 handcuffed me and dragged me out.

There were crowds of people standing around. I don't know who had called the police, but I ain't never seen them show up nowhere that fast before. The two officers roughly thrust me into the squad car.

"Yo, why the fuck ya gotta handle him like that? I told you, that shit was self-defense." In an effort to show support, Mel started talking crazy shit to the cops. Durty told Mel to chill, and tried to calm him down to keep him from getting arrested. The police started to ask questions, and just like in most 'hoods, when shit goes down, ain't nobody see nothing.

They started to search around outside for the weapon, since it was quite obvious I ain't beat Tone like that with my bare hands. Then, one of the police officers—a big, brawny, Rocky Balboa–looking Italian muthafucka, came over to the squad car where I sat and shouted "Where's the weapon at?"

"What weapon are you talking about, sir?" I responded.

The cop started to lose his patience real quick. "I see you wanna be a wiseass. Now I'll ask you one more time. Where is the weapon you used to bash that guy's skull in?"

"Fuck that nigga, Wa. Don't tell 'em shit!" Mel called out.

"Shut your mouth, before we take you in for obstructing an arrest," the officer barked at Mel.

"Where did you stash the weapon at, asshole!"

"I don't know what weapon you're talking about." I said again, sticking to my story.

"Okay. you wanna play hardball, you lying sack of shit?" The Rocky lookalike cop reached in and sucker punched me right in the stomach.

I gasped for air as I bent over in pain, with my hands still tightly cuffed behind my back.

"Uh-uh! Why the fuck you hit 'im like that?" I heard a female cry out. Then different voices yelled out after her, "That's my nigga right there! Y'all muthafuckas better not put your hands on him no more, or it's gon' be some shit!" Another voice screamed out some words of encouragement: "Hold your head up, baby boy."

Just as the cops had gathered up whatever information they could get, they started heading back to their cars.

"Man, fuck the police!" Mel called out belligerently. "Fam, I'ma do what I can to get you out. Don't worry 'bout nothing," he continued, as he turned towards the officer who assaulted me, "Fucking pigs," he spat out.

The big, mighty muscle cop made his way toward Mel. "That's it! Keep your fucking mouth shut or you're going down just like your friend here."

"Like I said, fuck you, pig!" Mel retorted defiantly. "You ain't taking me nowhere."

The officer's face turned tomato red and he charged at Mel.

As several of Mel's boys surrounded him like a shield, Mel's mom came running out her building and started cursing the cop out, "Uh-uh! Fuck that! That's my son right there. He the wrong one to fuck with, trust me. You touch him and I'll have your whole muthafuckin' precinct shut down, believe that! You can go around doing all that crooked shit to whoever you want, and get away with it. But you fuck with that one, I got my muthafuckin' video camera on Record in one of them muthafuckin' window up there. So, go ahead—make my day, you donut-eating bastard!"

Ms. Aubrey ain't play when it came to her children, especially Mel. The officer warily backed up towards his car and got in. As the other squad cars went their separate ways, my black ass was hauled off to the precinct.

ENYCHI

While I was at the shop unpacking boxes and pricing merchandise, I got a call from Denita. She was frantic and screaming at the top of her lungs.

"Denita, calm down! I can't hear you. What? Who? Oh my God!" When I finally made sense of what she said, I dropped my cell phone and stood there in shock.

Wasuan had killed Tone. My heart raced. All of sudden, I dropped to my knees and cried until I felt sick. When I couldn't cry no more, I sat in the middle of the floor and stared into space. I couldn't move and was filled with so much grief, I couldn't help but feel this was all my fault.

Although Tone and I were going through it, I never wanted to see him dead. *What about his daughters?* I knew this was going to devastate them.

I grabbed my keys, pulled the gates down on the store, locked it up, and went home. Tone was dead, and there wasn't nothing I could do for Wasuan right now. I sat on my couch, with tears once again running down my face, and thought about the two men in my life.

I thought about Tone and our trip to the Bahamas, him surprising me at the Benz dealer; and I'll never forget the day he blindfolded me and took me to the boutique and handed me the papers to sign. He had given me some of the finer things in life, the fancy restaurants, the shopping sprees, a lovely apartment. Everything a woman could ever dream of having, he made it possible for me to experience it, and for that I'll always be grateful to him. But when I thought about Wasuan, I remembered how we used to laugh together, sometimes for no reason at all, and how we often finished each other's sentences, we were so connected.

I thought about the day I had given him my virginity, his wide mouth smile, and how playful he could be at times. Wasuan was a lot of fun. We had a lot of first-time experiences together—embarrassing ones as well—like the time I was using a tampon for the first time, and somehow I inserted it wrong and couldn't get it out. Talk about panicking, I thought I was going to get an infection and die, but Wasuan came to my rescue and pulled that bad boy right on out. He cracked jokes about it for months, but I loved him for those up-close and personal moments we shared together.

My door buzzer interrupted my thoughts, so I got up and pushed the intercom button. "Who is it?"

"It's me, 'Nita! Open up!"

I buzzed her in, then walked over and opened the door. As soon as Denita appeared, I fell into her arms. " 'Nita, it's all my fault," I cried.

"Shh." Denita rubbed my back for comfort. "No, Enychi, it's not your fault."

I pulled back from her. "Did you get see Wasuan before

they took him to jail? What did Mel say happened? Do you think Wasuan went off because of what you told your brother?"

"Nah, I didn't even get a chance to tell him. The cops had already took by the time I got to my house. My brother did say that Wasuan was minding his business when Tone started disrespecting him, talking out about him being soft. That's when Wa lost it and started pistol-whipping the nigga," Denita said, with no remorse for Tone.

"What about Tone's body?"

"The coroners were bagging his body up as I was leaving."

"So he's really gone," I said, trying to wipe the tears from my face.

"Enychi, I know this is some crazy shit, but you have to pull yourself together."

"I know, at least long enough to go to Tone's funeral, to pay my respects." I paused, feeling lost.

Denita looked at me. "Enychi, you're taking crazy right now. You can't go to that man's funeral."

I stared at her in shock. "But—"

"It ain't no 'buts.' Listen to me girl. You know Tone's wife just lost her baby not too long ago, and now her husband. That's two people that *crazy* lost in less than a month, so just imagine what she's going through. Not that the bitch don't deserve every ounce of tragedy that come her way, but I'm saying you, Tone's quote-end-quote 'chick on the side,' try walking up in that funeral home? You in a room filled with all his wife's people, possibly her sisters, brothers, or even some of her cousins—his people—whoever. She gon' have a lot of emotions going, and I guarantee you, the sight of you is gonna set them off, because you was fucking her man.

"She already keyed up your car while the nigga was alive, *and* showed up to your house wanting to fight you while she was pregnant. Now, that bitch might pull out a razor, or something, and try to send *you* to an early grave over this shit. Trust me. I see it in the 'hood all the time, chick's be catching beatdowns, and getting hurt up bad, over some dead nigga that can't fuck neither one of their dumb asses no more. I'm telling you. That funeral shit, is not the place for a dead man's mistress to show up at."

I nodded. "You're right. I just wish I was able to pay my last respects to him."

"Enychi, what I'm about to say might sound coldhearted, but that's me. So here it go: Tone is dead now. Yeah, he came into your life and gave you nice shit, but he also threatened to take it back from you. So, fuck him; he served his purpose. Now it's time for you to move on, forget about Tone, his wife, and all that drama they was putting you through. Boo-boo, concentrate on you and your business—or should I say, *our* business? Shake that shit off, and let Tone's wife do the grieving, girl."

"Damn, Denita that is some cold shit to say! I *did* have a relationship with him, too!"

"Yeah, you had a little something going on, but I wouldn't call it a relationship. You was fucking him and he was paying for it. That's how the game's played. You wasn't the wife. You ain't gon' collect no death benefits, so put that nigga in the past. Anyway, look, you my girl and I love you, even if you are a little naive at times. So, do what you wanna do—except going to that funeral—a'ight? I'm gonna get ready to get up outta here, but if you need me call me, okay?"

"Okay, thanks for stopping by," I said, more than ready for Denita to get the hell out my apartment. But after she left I thought hard about what she said. I still wanted to pay my respects, but instead I said a silent prayer, just to let Tone know that I was gonna miss him.

WASUAN

From last night's stay in central booking, to this depressing-ass ride over to Rikers Island, I stared through the metal guards covering the windows of the rally wagon and asked myself the same mind-boggling question over and over again. *What made a real man?* Was it someone who valued his life and freedom enough to walk away from the uninterrupted troubles that tried to bring him down—even if it cost him his respect? Or was it someone who valued his respect enough to attack the troubles head-on—even if it cost him his life or his freedom?

I couldn't figure that one out, for the life of me. All I knew was that I was the one that had lost his respect by trying to avoid this trip right here. Now look at me: My life belonged to the fucking system.

I started to tear up as the C.O.s took me to intake to get processed.

During that processing shit, them fucking correction officers made you strip down butt-ass in a cold-ass room, while they watched your dick shrivel up. Then they ordered you to squat, spread your ass cheeks, open your mouth, cough, and lift up your fucking feet.

To me, that shit was worse than doing the fucking time. But it was too late to cry about it now. I knew that, if I made a deal with the devil, I eventually would have to pay the price.

After the search, I was handed my I.D. card, a pair of orange-canvas slip-ons, and—since my clothes was covered in Tone's blood—they gave me a gray jumper from the inmate visiting room. The C.O. escorted me to where I would be housed after I saw the judge. Unlike my last bid, this time it wasn't a cell all to myself. They placed me in a fuckin' dormitory with about fifty niggas on one side and another fifty on the other, and I definitely wasn't feeling that shit at all.

Dudes looked at me sideways as I walked alongside the wide-bootied female correction officer. Her badge identified her as Officer Hunter. "Wells, here's your assigned bunk," Officer Hunter said.

"We got another Queens nigga up in the house," some nigga yelled out. He must've been scoping me out real hard to see the first three numbers of my booking case number on my I.D. card. It had to be that, because every inmate's first three numbers were based on where they were from—Queens was number 441.

I sat down on the hard-ass cot and scanned the room for some familiar faces, but didn't see anyone I knew.

On one side of my bunk was a real young-looking Spanish dude, and on the other side was an old sickly-looking cat. He looked like life must've dealt him a bad hand. I seen that somebody must've given him the business, with that nice-size, buck-fifty slash running from his temple to his jawbone. Right then and there, he started coughing—one of them nasty, wheezing coughs. I just looked at that nigga like, *no the fuck they ain't put me next to dude.*

He caught my glare and said. "Hey there, young blood. I'm Nardo Williams. And you?"

He extended his hand and flashed a smile that revealed about six of his front teeth missing.

I looked down at his hand but didn't extend mine. "What's up, old timer? I'm Wa—Wasuan Wells. Is it cool to call you 'OT,' for old timer?"

He started his winded cough again before he answered "Yeah. You cool with 'young blood,' right?"

"I'm cool wit it." I nodded.

Several days later, I heard a wheezing voice slightly whisper, "Young blood, young blood, wake up," as the feel of a rough, parched hand shook me awake from my nightmare. It was OT.

"Oh shit! What—where am I?" I mumbled. I shook my head and cleared the sleep outta my eyes. I've had the same recurring nightmare about my pop's murder ever since I was a shorty. But this time it was different: I dreamt that I was beating Tone to death with the gun, but when I looked at his bloody face it wasn't Tone anymore, it was my pops. That shit was crazy to me. I woke up from one nightmare to live in another.

I been there on Rikers Island for a week, but this was a bigger nightmare than the ones that haunted me all these years.

"Must've had a bad dream, son." The voice was kind and reassuring. I looked around and saw only half of the hundred men in the room, so I wasn't quite as embarrassed as I would've been if all them niggas caught me having a bad dream. I guess the others had gone to morning chow.

"Yeah, I guess I did."

"Yeah, I know. I have a lot of those dreams myself." OT rocked back and forth, sitting on the edge of his cot.

"You do? What kind of dreams you talking, OT?"

"Young blood, you look like a good boy. I hate to see you in a place like this. Now, me on the other hand, shit, I was bad— bad to the bone—in my day. I did some horrible things."

I knew the unwritten law in prison was never to tell what you were in there for, so I never bothered to ask what he'd done.

OT went into a coughing fit before he could continue.

"You all right?" I asked.

He brushed off his coughing condition. "Don't worry about me, young blood. I know I ain't got much longer on this earth. I got the emphysema real bad. But I tell you one thing, some of those things I've done haunt me just like an evil ghost, and, so, I have them bad dreams, too."

"Oh yeah?"

"Yeah. We pay for everything we do in this life. There's no getting around it. I've got to say this 'fore I meet my maker, though. I killed somebody once and I never did any time for it, yet it has haunted me so much, I'll be glad when I finally close my eyes for good. It ain't so bad to kill somebody that ain't living right, but the dude I murdered was a pretty damn good dude."

"So, what are you in here for, if you don't mind me asking?"

"Nah, I' on mine. I'm in here for bank robbery. I'd gotten so strung out on that crack shit—bad, real bad." He coughed. "I thought I was invincible. You wouldn't know it to look at me now, but I used to be a high roller. Oh, I done lived me a life." He grinned with a missing- and brown-toothed smile.

I remained silent and studied him, watching the mood in his eyes change from one of remembered pride to one of true remorse.

He shook his head sadly. "Yessir. But if I had it to do again, there is some things I wish I could do different."

"Yeah, what's that OT?"

He paused for about thirty seconds, then he stood up, lifted his mattress, and pulled out a small raggedy, book. "Here—take this and read it," OT said in his out-of-breath tone, and he tapped on the book with his burnt-looking fingertip. "This right here is where you'll get your forgiveness from, young blood."

"Now, if I could do some things different—although there's many thangs I should've done different in my time—but the first thing I would've done is spared that man, my friend, his life. His murder is what made me start basing, because I couldn't cope with it no more; I had to get high, outta my mine so I couldn't feel, and was numb to everything that I couldn't or didn't wanna deal with. And his death was the main thing."

"Wow, yo, that's deep, man."

"No, that's real shit, true shit, young blood!" OT went into another coughing attack and, as I went to lay my head down to grasp and think about what he had just said, I heard a C.O. yell, "Wells, you got a visitor!"

"Aye, what up, baby?" Mel stood up and gave me a hug, once I was in the visiting area. "Yo, man, you a'ight? How you holding up?" he asked.

211

"I'm all right. Maintaining, to say the least, you know. I met this old head up in here. Me and him done got cool. So that nigga be trying to keep me sane for the most part, you know what I mean?"

"I hear that."

"Nah, but did you ever get my keys from Latavia so you can get that money out my safe for the lawyer?"

"Yo, man, I knew she was too cute to be on the up-and-up." Mel shook his head, "Man, that bitch is scandalous."

"What? Why you say that?"

"Yo, man, that bitch cleaned your shit out. Your TV gone— the stereo, too. I found the key to your safe, but that bitch took the fuckin' safe with her."

"Get the fuck outta here. Are you serious?"

"Yo, man. Dead serious. But, yo, your lawyer told me if you cop a plea, his fee is gonna be eight thousand, and if you take it to trial, it's gon' be twenty-five grand. But either way it go, I got you, nigga, a'ight? So, don't sweat that. But your girl, I got my people looking to do her ass dirty, if she ain't got your money."

"Whatever, 'cause she played me with that. Nah, I take that back: She played herself. Anyway, you seen Enychi since all this shit happened?" I changed the subject.

"Nah, the last time I saw her was when I checked out 'Nita's graduation. But I ain't say shit to her, though. I found out that, before that nigga Tone checked out, he bought her a little clothing store in Manhattan. Word up: She put my sister on as her partner. 'Nita said it's doing a'ight, too. They on some dressy, classy type shit. I think it's called . . ." Mel paused for a hot minute. "Umm, fuck it! I can't even remember the name of that shit."

"Oh, a'ight. That's what's up. I see that nigga must've really been feeling her, doing all that. I know she hate me now."

"Yo, man. Let that shit go, a'ight?"

"Nah, I'm cool. I just want her to be happy, and I know she was feeling dude, so—"

"Wells, your visit is up," the C.O. named Watts, sitting at the desk, yelled out before I could finish my sentence.

"Yo, man. I gotta go. But thanks for coming to check me, my nigga. I love you, man."

"Yeah, no doubt. Stay up, my nigga. I'ma see you again soon," Mel said as I departed.

■ You would think that after Tone's death Natalie would've been the least of my problems. Unfortunately, she was now my worst nightmare. Apparently, her version of what happened to Tone was slightly different from the truth. A week after Tone was killed, I was home alone stuffing my face with Ben & Jerry's Chunky Monkey ice cream, and still in mourning, while I watched *Why Do Fools Fall in Love*, the Frankie Lymon story, on DVD. *Frankie's three wives are something else.* I thought, and laughed.

When thinking of wives, my cell phone started to ring. I looked at the caller ID before answering. *Who the hell is calling me at ten o'clock at night from a blocked number?* I wondered. Since 'Nita was my only friend, and her ass was out with Rodney, I knew she wouldn't be calling. *Unless something happened*, I thought, considering the fact that Rodney's ass was always up to no good.

"Hello," I answered.

On the other end all I could hear was the voice of a woman screaming and crying. I couldn't quite make out what she was trying to say, but I could tell right away it wasn't Denita.

"Hello?" I repeated. "Miss, I think you got the wrong number."

"No, bitch! I got the right number." She stopped crying. "You had my fuckin' husband killed, didn't you, bitch? He told me he was gon' break it off with you, and this number was the last call he made on his cell phone. Now I'm hearing that some nigga you was fuckin' with killed him. You set him up, didn't you?" Natalie screamed.

"What! Look Natalie, I didn't have anything to do with that."

"You a lying-ass bitch, and when I see you, I'ma kill ya—"

I hung up on her before she could finish her threat. I couldn't believe that she was accusing me of setting Tone up. My cell phone started to ring again from a blocked number, and this time I cut my phone off. I wasn't about to fall for the same trick twice.

After that night, the drama continued. Natalie's psycho behind came to my apartment with two of her girlfriends. Someone must have let them in the building, because they were at my apartment door kicking and banging on it, like they were going to break it down. I acted like I wasn't home, but they must've saw the cover to the peephole move when I looked out of it, because Natalie kept yelling, "Bitch, I know you in there!"

Five minutes of sceaming and beating on my door, I heard a neighbors come out into the hallway and threaten to call the police it they didn't leave. As they were leaving, one of Natalie's girls said, "Fuck it, we'll catch her ass. She gon' have to come out of her apartment sooner or later."

I got up outta there a week after that incident. I moved into a co-op with a doorman, security guards, and cameras. Natalie still harassed me, calling my cell phone all times of the night and day, talking like she'd lost her mind for real. I entertained her and her silliness sometimes, arguing back and forth with her—until she started making promises to see me in the streets, and to have my boutique burned down. That's when all the game-playing stopped for me. From that point on, I saved all the reckless messages she left on my voice mail about killing me, and since a lot of my business connects had my number I couldn't just up and change it without notice so now I was ready to go to the police about Natalie, but Denita suggested we keep it street. Whatever that meant, I was with it, as long as it worked.

"Trust me, if Natalie loves them little girls of hers, my plan'll work," Denita assured me.

"Wait a minute, I ain't messing with Tone's kids, and neither are you!" I said, slightly raising my voice.

"E, be easy! I know that, but she don't know that. So, since she wanna make threats to destroy something we both hold dear, then we gonna do the same thing to her ass."

I'm glad we're friends, 'cause Denita was so devious at times. She got Rodney to call up Tone's wife and make threats to kidnap her babies and do all kinds of X-rated things to them, before sending them back to her in boxes—if she didn't leave me alone. By the time Rodney finished talking greasy to Natalie, the bitch was in tears.

Needless to say, that was that last of her!

W A S U A N

I had been going back and forth to court for the past couple of months. Mel got me this pretty sharp Jewish attorney named Reuben Dershowitz. He knew his stuff when it came to criminal law shit. So, him representing me had me feeling a little more relaxed. I knew I had to do the time for what I did, so I was mentally preparing myself for it. I just didn't wanna get lost in the system doing ten-to-twenty year bids, and Dershowitz said he was gonna put his best foot forward to see that that shit didn't happen.

Outside of my case, me and Old T was hanging out at chow together, and in the yard every day; and that nigga had some stories to tell. Although I felt kind of drawn to him, he wasn't my pops; he was just close in age. In fact, he wasn't nothing like my pops, because he devoted his life to crime, murder, and getting high, but he spoke on some pretty nifty tips he had for them crap games. Too bad I was never gon' roll them dice again.

But I liked Nardo, aka my friend OT. For some reason, I

felt a connection to his old ass. Speaking of connection, I got a
letter from my moms. I have to be honest, that was some shock-
ing shit, because I knew how dead set she was on not standing
by me up in this piece.

As I opened the envelope, my heart's ka-thump was about
double its normal speed—'cause I could just see hateful words
like "ashamed, less than a man, murderer" or maybe even her
saying that she hated me.

But once I started reading, I was comforted.

Dear Son,

*I don't really know where to start. I'm just going to say
what's in my heart. First and foremost, you need to know
that a mother's love is the greatest love, and although sometimes it may seem like I just gave up on you, I want you to
know you always stayed on my mind and in my heart. Mel's
mother kept me pretty up-to-date on as much as she knew
about what's going on with you.*

*However, I want to apologize for not keeping up with you
personally.*

*The day you showed up at my door, I felt like God had fi-
nally answered my prayers and that I was going to get a sec-
ond chance to be a part of your life. I know meeting Richard
might have been tough for you and caused you to stray again.
But after me and your father separated, I put off having a
social life so I could raise my son right. I didn't have a life
outside of being the best mother I could be to you. Your father's been dead for fifteen years now. Don't you think it's
time I have something for me that makes me happy? Well, I*

found that with Richard. So, I hope you can understand that. Just like I'm trying to understand and respect the decisions and choices you've made for your life. I love you, son, and I want you to know I'm here for you. I'm praying for you, and although I cannot and will not step foot in nobody's prison to visit my son, I will write you, or you can call me collect anytime, and if there is anything you need, I will do my best to see that you have it.

Take care, son, and please be careful in there.

I love you no matter what,

Love always,
Your mom, Vivian Wells

My mom's letter touched my heart, and it almost made me cry. Man, I swear, her words was right on time, 'cause knowing she ain't say "fuck you," or "I just give up on you," made my life seem a little more promising.

Plus, Mel visited on the regular, and he kept me feeling up. On his last visit, he had some good news, too.

Mel finally caught up with that bitch Latavia, and he came up on a visit to tell me about it. He said he saw her chilling with some wack-ass rapper dude, up in one of the VIP rooms at Jay-Z's 40/40 Club in Manhattan.

Mel laughed like a muthafucka as he continued on with the story.

"Yo, nigga, that bitch's timing couldn't have been better, 'cause at the time I was up in there with about eight bitches. Two was from Jersey, and the other six of them was from Brooklyn. And I ain't even gon' count the mob of niggas I had out with me that night. We was out celebrating our man Durty's twenty-fifth birthday in another VIP room, right next to the one Latavia's ass was in." Mel's laughing made his eyes water.

Between laughs he said, "First, niggas stepped to the dude she was with and asked him if he was feeling ol' girl enough to take a beatdown for her."

Mel was laughing so hard, I couldn't understand what the fuck he was saying.

"Come on, nigga. Tell the fuckin' story," I said, getting a little tight because I wanted to laugh about it right along with his ass.

"Okay. A'ight. I'm good now," he said, as he carried on. "Yo, man, the nigga was like, 'Yo, she cool and all that, but I just met this bitch, so, nah, I'm out.'

"Latavia's ass was standing there, shocked. And, since I ain't wanna disrespect my man Jigga's spot, we took the bitch outside and I gave her two options. One was, get me that money back she took from your crib, and two was, if not, I was gon' sick the pit bulls in skirts on her ass—all eight of them."

"Yo. Word. So what happened?" I asked 'cause the shit was getting good.

"Chill, nigga. Let me finish. She only had 35 Gs left. I got your stereo back from her ass, too. I ain't seen the TV, though; but after that, I still let them bitches loose on her ass, dawg! And, yo, when they got finished with that pretty yellow face of hers, the shit wasn't so pretty no more." Mel smirked. "Word. They put it on her like that."

"Like that, nigga?" I said. "You ain't feel bad about doing that? She did give back some of the money."

"Hell no, nigga. She gave *you* the pussy, not me. Besides,

that's your sensitive ass feeling sorry for a bitch. She ain't feel bad when she robbed you for your shit, knowing you was locked the fuck up and might need that money, did she?"

All I could say to that one was "You right, dawg. You right!"

ENYCHI

The drama was finally behind me, and my life was slowly getting back on track. On the business side, things had taken off rather quickly. Denita managed the boutique and also handled a bulk of the responsibilities, such as the orders from the distributors, the necessary paperwork, and the phone calls. I got tied up in sketching my designs and searching for the right fabrics for my upcoming clothing line, called Envy Me Couturier. Denita helped me come up with the name; each initial is the same as mine. I was definitely focused now, and the boutique's clientele was growing every day. My customers made such a big fuss over my designs, too.

As soon as I brought a new piece into the store, it sold that same day. Not that I expected anything less, but it felt good to know that they were really feeling my work. It got so busy at times that I barely had a moment to think.

Denita was damn near pulling her braids out because her patience was shot. But she was so good at managing the store—and we were working as partners with the clothing line as well. We planned to hit the fashion industry hard, with a series of

high-end designs. Now we were working on a name for Denita's
new clothing line—and she was loving all of the celebrity fashion shows and parties that we got invited to.

Denita's very outgoing. She loves the spotlight, which is
good for our business, because she really knows how to get up
into the hot spots and politic.

Me, I wasn't out anywhere, yet, because, when I was not at
the store, I was home creating new designs. Besides, I'm the laid-
back one. I wasn't that good with talking, but I know my shit,
and I make things happen. So, once Denita wheels 'em in, I get
'em hooked.

The social part of my life might have been a mess, but I was
so in love with my business, nothing else mattered. I knew I
owed a lot of my success to Tone. Purchasing this boutique for
me right in the heart of Manhattan's fashion district just made
all my dreams come true a lot sooner. So, I was always gon' be
thankul for that. And despite everything that had gone wrong
between us, I was grateful to Wasuan for everything he did for
me. He supported me while I was in school. He's the one that
really made this possible. Tone just put the finishing touches on
my dreams.

I thought about Wasuan often; I even tried to write him a
letter on a few occasions, but I was fighting too many feelings,
and I couldn't put the things I needed and wanted to say down
on paper, so I just scrapped the whole idea. Denita told me little
things she heard from Mel, like how he was holding up and
what not, but sometimes I just wanted to hear Wasuan say *"Enychi, ma, I'm good!"*

I've never been able to completely let him go. Even after
everything, he still has the key to my heart. Sometimes I think

it's because he was my first. That's funny though, because the other day this guy came into my boutique with his girl, wearing the same exact Scarface T-shirt that I woke up in the morning after Mel's New Year's party in 2003. As I look back at that and laugh, that shit wasn't so funny to me back then.

I remember opening my eyes from a deep, hungover sleep, once the sunlight started to seep through the windows' vertical blinds. I did an early morning stretch to shake off my drowsiness—before I looked around the room and suddenly realized that it wasn't mine. I remember looking down at the long, white T-shirt I was wearing—a T-shirt with a picture of *Scarface*'s Tony Montana sitting in front of a pile of cocaine, with a cigar in his mouth, and that's when I started to panic. As I quickly jumped up from the unfamiliar bed, I could feel the aftermath of the alcohol causing my head to pound in an excruciating and rapid pulse. I could remember having two or three cups of the red stuff at the party that night, but anything further than that was a blur. My recollection was definitely at a loss as to how I got where, who I was with, and what might of or could have happened.

With that in mind, the first thing I did was check to see if I still had my panties on. Then I stuck my hand inside of them to see if my coochie was suffering from any signs of discomfort. I was so relieved to find that everything was okay down there, I exhaled noisily. Next, I searched the room for my clothing, which was nowhere in sight. My eyes began to scan the room, as I grew curious about my surroundings. The black-and-gray comforter on the queen-size bed, along with the scattered men's clothing and large-size Timberland boots and sneakers all over the floor, was a dead giveaway that I was in a guy's room. Automatically, I began to beat up on myself for being so irresponsible.

Palming the side of my aching forehead, I stumbled over to the bedroom window and peeked out of the blinds. Through the window, I could tell I was in some type of apartment building, three stories up; but the outside scenery didn't give up enough detail to tell me where in the city I was. Inside, the apartment was silent; and even though I was afraid of what might be waiting on the outside of that bedroom, I felt it was best to take my chances, hoping that maybe I would find a phone, or even better, my clothes, and make a run for the door.

As I hesitantly tiptoed from the bedroom into a short hallway that led to the nicely furnished living room, I heard the rattling sound of keys, which forced me to run back to the room. I could hear the ka-thumping sound of my racing heart, as my body started to tremble. Nervously, I paced around the room. I didn't know who was about to enter the bedroom, or whether or not I might have to fight my way up out of there, as I heard a door slam and the sound of footsteps moving closer towards the bedroom door. For a moment, I thought about hiding in the small closet packed with clothes, or even under the bed—but there were too many thoughts running through my mind at one time, and not enough time to decide which one was best.

Quickly, I grabbed up the bottle of cologne that sat on the night table next to the bed. Thinking, O*kay, I'll spray him in his eyes, kick 'im where it hurts, and make a run for the door*. As my deciding option, I braced myself slightly behind the bedroom door with my finger on the pump of the bottle, and waited for the door to open—when in walked Wasuan, holding my clothes

all cleaned up from the vomit I got on them, and nicely folded
in the crook of his arm. I let out a hard sigh of relief when I saw
that it was him. But when I stepped from behind that door, boy,
did he let me have it about how drunk I had gotten and what
could've happened if he hadn't looked out for me. We went
back and forth about it for a minute, because I couldn't believe
I'd wild-out like that . . . well, let's just say I didn't want to believe it. I was so embarrassed that all I could do was ask where
the bathroom was.

I stared sheepishly at myself in that bathroom mirror, I was
so ashamed about the whole ordeal. *How could you behave so irre-
sponsibly?* I asked myself over and again, as my migraine got
worse. I opened Wasuan's medicine cabinet, hoping to find something to help the splitting headache, but unfortunately, all I saw
was toothpaste, floss, and razors. Suddenly, a light knock on the
door interrupted my search.

"Yes," I answered, as I fumbled to quietly close the cabinet.

"I thought you might need your purse, your shoes, and a
washcloth—just in case you wanna wipe your face off," he said,
as he stood on the other side of the bathroom door.

I stood behind the door so I couldn't see Wasuan's face, as
I cracked it just enough for him to slip my belongings
through, and then I swiftly closed it back. I looked in my purse
to find that everything was in place. Only, the battery on my
cell phone had died. I wondered if Denita had tried to call me.
Just thinking of her—she had cut out on me without saying a
word that night—I was angry. When I slipped into my pants, I
noticed my lace, Victorian-style blouse, from Bebe, that it
took me a month to save up for, was ruined. It was a dry
clean–only, and apparently Wasuan had *washed* the shirt and

put it in the dryer. I was so pissed. I tossed the blouse in the wastebasket and stormed out of the bathroom, still wearing Wasuan's Scarface T-shirt.

Yeah, I can laugh at that now—and I *was* glad to see it was Wasuan that walked in the door that morning. After that we were inseparable. I can't help but smile when I think about our relationship, and sometimes I wonder what it would've been like if none of the drama had happened between us and we were still together; but once I thought about Wasuan's excessive gambling habits, I couldn't imagine it would've ever worked out.

Now I had to deal with Denita constantly in my ear about how I needed to get out more and start dating again. The dating part I wasn't ready for, but after a while I finally let Denita talk me into into going to Iso Life's annual party out in the Hamptons. I must say, I was actually excited about attending this event, because, not only was Iso Life doing big things in the fashion industry, but I was a huge fan of the designer's unique and exotic creations for his sherling-and-leather outerwear.

The night of the party, Denita volunteered to drive, since Mel helped her purchase a silver Lexus GX, with black leather interior. I was happy for her, and even happier that she was gonna do that two-hour drive to Hamptons. That is, until she got on my case about me wanting to hold off on dating.

"Enychi, you know it's gonna be some fine-ass niggas up in there tonight, right?" Denita said.

"Denita, please don't start!"

"What? I'm starting, 'cause, damn, how long you plan to bury yourself into work? You know what they say about all work and no play?"

"No, 'Nita, I don't know what they say, but I have heard the saying that hard work pays off. So, when I'm sitting on some real money, living in a house, and my business starts to branch off, then I'll party more, and maybe even date. Besides, this is the first time I've been independent and single in almost three years, so right now I just need to do me."

"I understand what you're saying, but you don't have to be in a relationship to have a little fun and get yourself a little dick every now and again."

"I know, but I ain't trying to run around having casual sex with this nigga and that nigga. I'm straight. I don't need the headaches. Next thing I know, another bitch will be looking for me, saying I was fucking her man, so she gon' blow up my store." I laughed.

"Yeah, that bitch Natalie must of lost her fucking mind when she lost that baby and that no-good-ass nigga Tone."

"Denita, stop it, now, you know that ain't nice."

"It might not be, but it's true. Shit, that nigga wasn't shit, but he did lace you, though, I will give him that. But on the real, Enychi, he gone now, so you can tell me the truth?"

"The truth about what, 'Nita?"

"You was in love with that nigga Tone, wasn't you?"

" 'Nita, I've only been in love once, and you know who that person was. I really liked Tone in the beginning, but I never felt the kind of connection I had with Wasuan. But they both turned out to be wrong for me."

"Yeah, girl, you sure do know how to pick 'em. But, you know Wasuan about to get sentenced in a couple of weeks, right?"

"Nah, I didn't know that." I got lost in my thoughts for a

moment before I came clean about my true feelings. " 'Nita, I know Wasuan did me dirty, but I still love him, and it has nothing to do with Tone being gone, because I felt this way while Tone was alive. There was nothing Tone could do to make me stop loving Wasuan. It's like there's this void in my life that only he can fill."

"Damn, that is deep. You must love that nigga Wasuan for real, if you can still feel that way about him after he did you like that. But people make mistakes and learn from them. So maybe you should write him, tell him how you feel. I mean, he's locked up, Tone is dead, and you're the one that came out on top, so fuck the past! Go for it, if that's what'll make you happy. You already have his address."

"Thanks for the advice, 'Nita!" I smiled.

"Uh-huh. Just promise me you'll have some fun tonight."

"I will," I said, wearing a smirk on my face.

When we arrived at the mansion where the party was being held at, it only made me dream bigger. It was in a gated community, and the landscaping was like nothing I'd ever seen before. And then I stepped onto the shiny marble floors, all black, beige and outlined in gold. The unfurnished mansion was huge, and the crowds of people that was stepping up in there was filling the place up quickly. I watched attentively as the models sashayed across the floor wearing Iso's latest designs, thinking to myself *Yeah, this is exactly how I'm plan to be doing things real soon.*

Outside of fashion, I let my hair down and had quite a few drinks, danced a little, and even took a couple numbers just to

satisfy Denita, but I had no intention on calling either one of
them. However, I had such a good time that I actually started to
hang out a little more. Unfortuantly, it got repetitive, and at
every party I saw the same tired-ass guys spitting the same
tired-ass rap.

WASUAN

Being in jail was getting to me. And the hard part about it was that my time hadn't even started yet. Between the bad dreams at night and the constant regrets during the day, I wished I would've, or could've, played my cards differently. This kept running through my mind daily, and I felt restless. I questioned my fate a lot, because I never was the type to get into a fight, let alone take another man's life. I really just wanted to be with my girl, shoot a little c-lo every now and again, and live my life as straight and narrow as possible. I never meant to kill nobody.

So why did I kill Tone? I asked myself that question every single day. I knew it wasn't self-defense; it wasn't 'cause he was with my girl, neither. I think the only reason I did it was to prove to myself that I was a man. A real man. 'Cause I ain't feel like one since I allowed myself to ask Enychi to fuck with that nigga Tone. That's when every ounce of man ran away from me. I had all the *if onlys* in the world, but I don't believe I regret killing Tone, because in my heart I felt, if it wasn't for me getting him first, that nigga would've eventually did away with me.

Most of my life, I really believed that I had the spirit of a hustler pouring out of my soul, but now that I done gambled too many times and lost big, it was time for me to set that nigga free.

I got into another deep discussion with my man OT, and this time I opened up to him about what I did to get in this hellhole. I even shared with him those nightmares that I'd been having, from witnessing my pop's murder when I was ten. Of course, he hit me with some more shit to think about when he said, "I just want you to know, young blood, when you take a life, you carry that life with you the rest of your long live days. I've had that nightmare all my life. And if there's anything I can tell you, blood, is to try to get out of here and turn your life around, 'cause you can't beat them streets. Ain't nobody ever beat the streets.

"I often wonder whatever happened to the family of the dude I killed. Now, I know what I did, and I know how that must've affected them." He heaved a deep sigh. "And more than anything, I want them to know how truly sorry I am. And I just hope that maybe they can find some forgiveness in their hearts for me and what I did. That's all I ever wanted, young blood."

Later that night, I woke up to the sounds of OT wheezing, gasping, and panting like I never heard him do before. He clutched his chest.

"Hold on, old timer! Yo, C.O.! Guard! Officer Watts! Somebody help!" I yelled "Don't die on me, man, don't go." Tears escaped from the corners of my eyes.

"Sorry . . . ," OT struggled to say—before he died in my arms.

As they carried his dead body out of the dormitory, with the cover pulled over his head, I heard one of the inmates say "That nigga Gunz finally kicked the bucket. He used to be a bad-ass muthafucka back in the days. Shit, that nigga sported a different Cadillac every day. I looked up to him, too, until he lost his swagger and started getting high—wanting to rob and kill muthafuckas. Oh, well, rest in, nigga!"

I stood under the shower, wishing the water would just wash away my pain, thinking about all the fucked-up decisions and poor judgments of my past, I've made so many.

I'd been battling with my emotions for too long, and I couldn't fight it no more.

This last incident put the icing on the cake. I was experiencing so many mixed emotions that I didn't know how or what to feel.

In my heart, I felt like I had betrayed my pops by befriending his fuckin' killer, Gunz. What hurt me was that I actually started to care for the nigga, as if he was a father to me. And all along that nigga was the reason I no longer had one.

I shed tears for him, held him in my arms, and even tried to help his ass breathe when he was dying. Now I wish he could've lived so I could've killed him myself.

But on the outside looking in, when I listened to him express his remorse and regret for the man he killed, and how he wished he could have just told the man's family how he was sorry, I can't lie—I felt for him, and hoped he could get the family's forgiveness so he could be at peace with himself. But now that it turned out that my pops was the man he killed, and I was the one whose forgiveness he was seeking, that shit was hard for me to grasp onto.

Thinking about all the hate I had for Gunz all these years made me come to terms with something else I didn't realize before. The same hate I had for the man that killed my father was the same hate Tone's children would feel towards *me* for the rest of their lives—and having that on my heart was gon' eat away at me just like it ate away at Gunz.

So, who was I to judge Gunz, when I was just like him? I killed a man without thinking about the pain I would cause that man's family, and, just like Gunz, one day, maybe sooner than later, I would seek forgiveness from his children and his family as well.

Right then and there, I asked God for forgiveness; and as I struggled to forgive myself, I looked to my Maker for some assistance.

For the first time, I opened the Bible that Gunz had gave me. Somehow, the Bible fell open to Proverbs 9:6: "Forsake the foolish, and live; and go in the way of understanding."

From that point on, I felt that God had spoken to me, because my life started to change. I read and studied my Bible every day, and I even began to attend Sunday services inside.

For the first time ever, I had something that I never had before: I had faith in the Man up above. And with that, I knew everything was going to be all right.

Finally, after six months of deliberating and going back and forth to court, it was time for my sentencing. Mentally, I had prepared myself for some serious time, and at this point, I was ready to take my punishment for what I had done.

My lawyer came to visit me the morning before I was due in court, just to prep me and give me a heads up on what kind of time they was talking about.

As I walked into the courtroom in shackles, I couldn't help but smile on the inside. *What a surprise!* I said to myself. Sitting in the room, I saw my homie through thick and thin, Mel, and his moms. Tears came to my eyes. I know that throughout this ordeal I had had a lot of tears, but these were happy ones. Sitting next to Ms. Aubrey was my moms and her boyfriend Richard, and I felt every bit of their love and support in that courtroom. Thank you, God. Right where I stood, I gave praise.

With that, I stood before Judge Dicks.

"How does the defendant plead for the murder of Anthony Jarod Myers?"

"Your Honor, my client, Wasuan Wells, pleads guilty."

Judge Dicks turned to me. "How do you plead?"

"Guilty," I said.

"I hereby sentence you to seven years firm imprisonment for the charge of voluntary manslaughter. You will be placed back in state custody immediately. Court is adjourned."

After the hearing ended, I turned to my mom, whose tears were escaping her eyes, and I lip-synched to her *I love you, Ma.*

"I love you, too, son," my mother mouthed back at me, as her boyfriend wrapped his arms around her and consoled her.

Later, I sat on my bunk reading my Bible. I thought about everything that happened in my life, and it hit me. My life had already been written before I was born. I also thought about

Tone's life, and even though I was working towards forgiveness, I still felt like I was just given a slap on the wrist for his murder.

To me, society was mixed up. There were men in prison doing twenty-five years for selling drugs. Now don't get me wrong. I know that's murder, too—just a slow form. But to me, for the users, it was still death by choice. In my case, I took a man's life without giving him a choice to live, and all they gave me was seven years, with no time knocked off for for good behavior?

I stopped in my tracks to think about that statement for a moment, then smiled as I realized that my slap on the wrist ain't come from no judge, or from society, or from the DA, it came from God.

I flipped back to the first page I ever came across when I opened the Bible, Proverbs 9:6. The message was, *Leave your impoverished confusion and live! Walk up the streets to a life with meaning.*

"Wasuan Wells, you have a visitor."

I looked up and tucked my Bible up under my mattress, thinking, "Wow, my man Mel." I didn't expect to see him, since he came to court today.

I headed over to officer. Cox, as he escorted me to the visiting room. "You know who my visitor is, Officer Cox?" I knew the chances of my mother visiting me was real slim, but anything was possible.

"Nah, but you'll see," Cox responded.

"Table Twelve," Officer Gibbs said.

As I scanned the room for table 12, I froze dead in my tracks.

"Wells, have a seat, table Twelve," Officer Gibbs demanded.

I slowly approached my table, not knowing what to say, think, or expect.

Enychi stood up, wrapped her arms around me, and started to cry.

At first, I thought maybe something tragic had happened, like her mother dying, or something to that effect. I couldn't understand why she would come here to see me. Mel told me she was doing real good for herself.

Finally, I embraced her. My heart was pumping hard and fast, as I pulled away from her so we could sit down and talk. I was defiantly curious to know why she was here.

"Hey, umm, you okay?" I was nervous.

"I'm sorry. I knew exactly what I wanted to say to you before I got here, but now I can't seem to find the words," Enychi said.

I looked at her face as the tears continued to flow. Man, she was still so beautiful. She looked like she'd picked up a little weight, but it was all in the right places. She also had cut the front of her hair and wore bangs now, with the rest of it nice and long down the side of her face, and hanging below her shoulders.

"Well, Enychi. Since you don't know where to start, I just wanna start by saying that I'm sorry for everything wrong that I did to you. I'm sorry for getting addicted to the gambling; I'm more than sorry for allowing Tone to come into your life, and for taking him out your—"

"Please, Wasuan. I'm not here to talk about the past," she said, cutting my words short.

"Okay. Well, how are things going with you?" I decided to go for small talk.

"Besides the empty space that's in my heart, I'm getting by pretty well." For a moment, neither one of us spoke. I never imagined an awkward moment like this between us.

"Umm. I know what that empty feeling in your heart feels like, because I've been trying to get used to the feeling for a while now."

Enychi started to cry hard, as she buried her face in her hands. I reached over the table we were sitting at and tried to console her, as I rubbed my hand across her back. "Enychi, whatever you're going through, God will see you through. It's gonna be all right."

"No, it won't be all right. I can't go on like this!"

"Like what, Nych?"

"Hiding what I feel. I can't keep doing it."

"Look. I know you gotta hate me, Enychi, that's why it's important to me that you know how truly sorry I really am."

"Wasuan, I wish I could hate you, but I can't. I don't. After all that we've been through, I still love you and always have."

My mouth dropped wide open. I couldn't believe my ears. "What?" I needed to hear her say that again.

"Wasuan, I'm still in love with you. No matter how hard I try to tell myself that I'm not, I can't get over you. I love you, Wa. I want us to forget the past and work on our future together."

Shocked, I sat back in my chair and rubbed my hand across my chin.

"What's wrong? You don't love me anymore? If not, I understand, Wasuan." Enychi put her head down and rubbed her hand across the table like she was brushing something off of it.

"No, I do, Enychi; but it's not that simple. You see where I'm at? Well, I'm gon' be here for seven years, Enychi. Seven years. I can't have you waiting for me for that long. Find yourself a good dude that can take care of you, be there for you, and treat you right. Please, just move on with your life."

"Wasuan, I don't need to be taken care of, and I've tried moving on, but my heart won't let me. Why can't you understand that, without you, I don't have a life? I don't care if you have to do a hundred years. I wanna do it with you."

"Enychi, what about—"

"No, Wasuan, what about nothing. Do you still love me, Wasuan?"

"You know I do, Enychi."

"Wasuan, I need to hear you say you do."

"Enychi, I love you with all my heart. I know I messed things up with us, but I've always loved you. I never stopped."

"Okay, so if we both feel the same way, Wasuan, then why shouldn't we be together? I'm here for you, and I'm ready to be whatever you need me to be."

"For real? You sure you serious?"

"Yes. Yes. I've never been more serious in my life."

I couldn't help but smile. God is definitely good. "Okay, baby. Let's do it then."

Enychi leaned over and wrapped both her arms around me,

and we sealed the deal with a sloppy, wet, and passionate lip lock.

And, ahh, man, did I miss kissing them lips; but just as I was getting into it I heard "Wells, your visit is up."

EPILOGUE

"Wasuan Wells, let's go," the officer said, as he opened my cell gate.

Yeah, it was that time.

Those seven years were rough, but I spent all of my time working, doing a lot of reading, and getting in shape. I'd put on thirty pounds of muscle and was in good health. I did what I had to to keep busy and stay out of trouble. And, of course, the love and support from my loved ones on the outside made the bid a lot easier. My moms remarried. Richard wasn't a bad guy after all. We've talked, and he even came up to visit me quite a few times during my seven-year stretch. He truly loves my mother, and he makes her happy—so how could I not be happy for her?

Mel was still keeping up with me, too. My boy opened up a couple of car-detailing shops, moved his moms, Ms. Aubrey, out of the projects and into a condo, and he finally retired from the drug game. Denita finally let Rodney go and got engaged to a football player from the New England Patriots. She's still a regular party head, but her and Enychi now own a multimillion-dollar business.

As I got nearer to the prison exit, I felt as excited as when I was being released from jail after doing my first bid ten years ago. Only, this time around my heart pounded like it was gon' bust out my chest, and the excitement I was feeling was like nothing I'd ever felt before, because I knew that once those gates to the outside opened, it was gon' be something more beautiful than sunshine waiting to greet me. And, sure enough they opened, and there she was, my sunshine, my beautiful wife, Enychi Michelle Wells, standing at the gate, waiting for me to walk out.

That's right, it was official! I made her my wife for real, a month after she came to see me those seven years ago. As soon as she saw me, she smiled real big, and the tears began to fall from her face.

"Hey, baby," Enychi cried, as she ran into my arms. "Oh, I'm so glad it's over and you can come home."

Then I heard our four-year-old baby boy cry out, "Daddy, Daddy, pick me up!" I smiled proudly as I picked up my son and he wrapped his little arms around my neck and said, "Daddy, me and Mommy taking you home, right?"

"For sure," I answered my li'l man.

"Here, Daddy, this one's for you," Enychi hit a button on the car key and handed it to me. The doors on the 2011 BMW opened by themselves, and the car spoke: "Hello. Please get in and fasten your seat belts."

I was amazed with the car, but nothing amazed me more than how my life had turned out. God is good! Through it all, I ended up marrying the love of my life, had a beautiful baby boy, and was the happiest man alive. So, who said love can't conquer all!